"I don't have to listen to this," Kim fumed. She glanced at me, as if waiting to see if I'd defend her. But after her backstabbing comment earlier, there was no way I was speaking up for her. Or Taylor. And certainly not Bri. I was done with all of them.

So I whirled around, tugged Mr. S's leash, and stalked toward home. A small part of me hoped that my friends would call me back, would finally say that they'd realized I was right.

But all I heard behind me was each of my friends stomping off alone.

Roxbury Park ✺ D🐶g Club

Roxbury Park Dog Club

A BONE TO PICK

DAPHNE MAPLE

HARPER
An Imprint of HarperCollinsPublishers

Roxbury Park Dog Club #6: A Bone to Pick

Text by Daphne Maple, copyright © 2017 by HarperCollins Publishers

Illustrations © 2017 by Annabelle Metayer

www.harpercollinschildrens.com

Library of Congress Control Number: 2016930380

ISBN 978-0-06-237102-7

Typography by Jenna Stempel

16 17 18 19 20   OPM   10 9 8 7 6 5 4 3 2 1

First Edition

For Betsy

1

The halls of Roxbury Park Middle School were packed with kids talking and laughing as I wove my way toward my best friend Kim's locker. That was our official meeting place after the last bell rang every day and today I was running a little late.

"Hi, Sasha," Kim said when I finally made it.

"Let's get going," my other best friend, Taylor, said with an easy grin as she slung her bag over her shoulder.

It was so bulky and heavy it took her two tries. "I don't want to be late for class." Taylor, who was the newer of my best friends, took fabulous pictures and had just started studying advanced photography at the Roxbury Park Art Center.

"And I'm helping my mom out at the Pampered Puppy today, so I should hustle too," Bri said.

Bri was the newest member of our pack and in some ways I was still getting to know her. She was also the newest member of the Roxbury Park Dog Club, which Kim, Taylor, and I had founded at the start of the year. Seventh graders at Roxbury Park Middle School were required to do community service and the three of us had signed up to work at the local dog shelter, an amazing place that took in homeless dogs and kept them safe and happy until they found new homes. But Alice, who ran the shelter, was having trouble making ends meet. At the same time, Kim's neighbors were looking for someone to walk their dog, Humphrey, in the afternoons before they got home from work. In a flash of brilliance Kim realized that if we started a dog club after school at the shelter, dogs could get a few hours of much needed exercise and fun, and we could bring in some extra money for the shelter. Many of the dogs' owners also signed up for pickup service, which meant we'd swing by their homes on the way to club meetings and walk the dogs to the shelter. It cost a bit extra but was worth it for owners who were busy at work.

"Did you guys get that email from Alice last night?" Kim asked. "The one with a picture of Coco in her new home?" The big black and brown dog had been one of our earliest club members and I was sad to see her go, but the picture last night had definitely showed us all how happy she was.

"She's living the doggy dream," Taylor said, making us laugh. Coco's owner had moved to a big farm in Pennsylvania, with acres of land to run on and lots of ducks and squirrels to chase. It really was the doggy dream and I was happy Coco got to live it.

"We have to figure out how many new dogs we can

take into the club now that Coco's gone," Kim said as the four of us walked toward the door.

The club had been a huge success, especially after we'd been featured in the local newspaper with pictures taken by Taylor. Now we had a wait list and Alice had been able to start up a new venture, a foster program for dogs. We were all huge fans of that project, but it definitely kept Alice busy.

"How many club dogs are there now?" Taylor asked as we walked down the front path of the school. Kids milled around us and a football whizzed past between a pair of eighth graders.

"Popsicle, Jinx, Waffles, Missy, Hattie, and Humphrey," Bri said as she ticked off on her fingers. Sometimes it still surprised me that Bri was a club member. Not so long ago she'd been mean to Taylor, jealous that Taylor had been the new girl but fit in so seamlessly. To make matters worse, Bri's mom, who owned a fancy doggy day care, had tried to take our club down. For a while their aggressive advertising plan had worked, but in the end we all realized that there was room in town for two dog care centers. At the same time Bri realized that Taylor was awesome while Taylor, with her big heart, realized Bri just needed friends. Bri began hanging out at the shelter and loved it so much that we asked her to join the club. "Plus Daisy and Gus—and of course Mr. S and Lily." She shot me a grin when she said the last two names and I grinned right back. Bri and I had both adopted shelter dogs, and they loved going back to visit their pals.

My parents got divorced when I was little, so it was just me and my mom, which could get a little lonely. Bringing Mr. S home had totally fixed that, and I adored my snuggly Cavachon with all my heart. Lately he'd been taking up a lot more of my time though. Mr. S was an older dog and as a result needed to go out more often. Of course I always took him—I needed my sweet pup comfortable, and my mom, who was a bit of a neat freak, did not want an accident in the house. But with everything else I had going on, the extra walks were tough.

"That's ten club dogs," Kim said. The brisk wind whipping the fall leaves off the trees had turned her cheeks pink. Winter was not far off and I was glad I'd worn my thick green fleece. I didn't want my muscles to get cold on the walk over to dance rehearsal. My mom used to drive me, but she was extra busy at work right now and it really wasn't a long walk to the studio.

"I think we could take in two more dogs since there are four of us plus Tim and Caley," Kim continued. Tim and Caley were high schoolers who volunteered at the shelter with us. At first it had been a little intimidating to work with older kids, but now we were all really comfortable together. "And that would bring our total to twelve club dogs."

"That sounds good," Taylor said, smoothing down her braids. Despite her efforts, the beads at the ends were clinking musically in the wind.

"So you'll call the next people on the wait list?" Bri said to me in her direct way. Even though she worked hard to control her temper, there were still times when she was blunt in a way that could sting. I knew this wasn't one of those times: handling new clients was part of my job at the club, so of course she'd ask me about it. But it still made my stomach tighten up because I really did not have time to call anyone, let alone a family from the wait list who would have a ton of questions and take ages to schedule for their trial visit.

"I'll try to get to it tonight if I have time," I said, absently twisting a curl around my fingers. Bri and I were both wearing our long hair in ponytails but mine was sloppy, with curls leaking out, while Bri's straight black hair was sleek, with a few carefully curled strands framing her face. She was twisting the jade charm she always wore on a red string around her neck—Bri was Chinese American and she had told us that the pendant was for good luck.

"We're all going to be pretty pressed for time with that report we have to do for social studies," Kim said with a sigh as we waited for a car to pass before crossing Market Street. Kim struggled in school and recently her

7

parents had considered sending her to private school. Eventually they'd agreed to let her stay with us at Roxbury Park Middle School but it was on the condition that she keep her grades up. Tutoring sessions with Taylor's math genius older sister, Anna, helped a lot, but Kim still got anxious, especially when we had big assignments. And the cultural essays that Mr. Martin had announced today were definitely intimidating. That was a big reason I was so stressed, too—I had no extra time, so how was I supposed to write ten pages about Mongolia, a country I knew nothing about?

"I wish he'd let us choose the place we were studying," Taylor said. "I'd rather learn about Egypt or France than Iceland."

"I think Iceland is partly covered by glaciers," Bri said. She'd lucked out with Italy. She could write about yummy food and the painting on the ceiling of the Sistine Chapel, and she'd be done in no time, unlike the rest of us. "That could be cool to write about."

"I need to find something interesting like that about

Tanzania," Kim said. Her cheeks were now pale, a sure sign she was feeling anxious.

"I think they have lions there," I said, remembering something my mom had said about endangered species. She had started an environmental law firm where Taylor's dad worked too and she liked talking about her cases. "You could write about that."

"Lions are definitely cool," she said thoughtfully. "Okay, maybe this report won't be so bad."

If only there were lions in Mongolia.

"Yeah, I don't think it will be that big a deal," Bri agreed. "And Sasha, I don't think calling families on the wait list will take that long. We don't want people waiting forever and not hearing from us."

I felt a slight flash of irritation at her pushiness. That was total Bri, of course, and I liked it when she was pushing to help the dogs or telling an eighth grader to give us space in the hall. But it wasn't so great when it felt like she was nagging me.

"We know you're busy practicing for your

performance though," Kim said, smiling at me and cheering me right up. Dogs and dance were my two favorite things and when I wasn't at our club, I was at the dance studio, where I took three classes a week as a member of the junior company. Our first big recital was coming up in a few weeks, so I was extra busy with rehearsals, especially since I had a solo in our jazz number.

"We'll be in the front row," Taylor promised. "I can't wait to see you do your thing."

It was funny to think that Taylor had only moved here from North Carolina this summer since it felt like I'd known her forever. Kim had been coming to my shows for years and always brought me a bouquet of pink roses, my favorite. But this would be the first time Taylor and Bri would be there and I was excited. And a little nervous—I had a lot of work to do if I wanted to be ready. "I'm glad you guys will be there," I said. "But it *is* going to keep me pretty busy."

"Yeah, that makes sense. I can't wait to see you

perform either," Bri said immediately, the warmth in her voice wiping away the last traces of the annoyance I had felt.

"Do you get to wear a really cool costume?" she went on.

And her words made me realize something that froze me in my tracks, like my shoes were suddenly glued to the ground.

"What's wrong?" Kim asked, seeing the expression on my face.

"I forgot my dance bag at school," I gasped. I could picture exactly where it was, on the hook at the back of my locker. I'd planned to grab it last, but then I'd gotten distracted debating whether I needed to bring home my science binder and now, instead of hanging from my shoulder, it was still dangling in my empty locker.

"Can you dance without your stuff?" Taylor asked, her brown eyes full of concern.

"No," I said, taking a deep breath. "I have to go back for it. I'll see you guys later."

My friends called good-bye as I took off running back toward school. But I knew no matter how fast I went I was going to be late for class and Madame Florence, my dance teacher, was not going to be pleased at all.

It was not a good start to the afternoon!

2

By the time I arrived at dance everyone was halfway through warm-ups. I could hear the familiar music and the sound of Madame Florence's voice leading everyone through the usual stretches as I ran into the dressing room to yank my leotard, jazz pants, and jazz shoes on. Usually the dressing room, with its rows of benches and lockers, was where I shifted gears from school to dance, getting in what Madame Florence called "a dance mind-set." But today I was too frantic to think about anything but hurrying.

"Mademoiselle Brown, you are late," Madame Florence said when I finally made it into the studio. I was panting from all the running I'd done to get here and despite the cool fall day, my temples and the back of my neck were sticky with sweat.

Madame Florence took all of this in with an arched brow of disapproval. "Your muscles look tight," she said. "Take a few extra minutes to relax before beginning your warm-up."

I nodded obediently, then walked in slow circles, staying out of the way of my classmates, who were all at the far side of the room. I loved the big dance room at the studio, with its soft pink walls and gentle lighting, and the beautiful Degas prints of ballerinas decorating the walls. Being there calmed me down and helped me focus, but it still took almost fifteen minutes to limber up my body enough to dance.

"We have already practiced the dance with your

solo," Madame Florence informed me. There was a coolness to her tone that wasn't usually there when she spoke to me and it made my chest clench up. I hated when people were angry at me. "We do not have time to go through it again, so you will stay after to run through it with me, yes?"

I nodded so hard my ponytail slapped the back of my neck, even though I knew that staying late would upset my mom. But how could I refuse Madame Florence when she was asking me to do something to make up for my lateness? Plus I really needed the rehearsal time. I decided I'd just do my best to be fast and skip changing back into my school clothes when we were done.

But even so, by the time I flew down the steps to my mom's waiting car, still in my sweaty dance clothes, she had been waiting for me for a while.

"So you forgot your dance bag again?" she asked with a sigh after I'd explained the delay. We drove down Main Street, the small stores and restaurants golden in the light of the setting sun. She said it like it happened every day instead of just one other time before. Well, maybe a few more if you counted the times I'd forgotten it at home in the morning and had to come back for it before school. But it wasn't like it happened *all* the time.

"Yeah, but I'll be more careful about remembering it from now on," I said, shifting a little in my seat. Usually I felt relaxed and all stretched out after dance but the frown on my mom's face had my muscles tightening up. Even passing Sugar and Spice, the candy store I loved, and the Rox, the diner Kim's family owned, didn't make me smile like it usually did.

"You said that the last time," my mom pointed out. She was like Bri when it came to straight talk and I winced at her words.

"I think I'll put it on the same hook as my backpack so I really can't leave it behind," I said. We'd passed through downtown and were now driving along Spring Street, almost at our house.

Finally my mom smiled at me. "That sounds like a good plan," she said.

And now I could sit back against my seat and feel the calm that came after the hard workout of a dance class.

Unfortunately though, it was short lived.

"Can you put water on for pasta while I change out of my work clothes?" my mom asked as we walked up the front path to our house. We lived in a pretty Victorian and my mom made sure the lawn was always mowed and the flower beds were weeded.

"Sure," I said. But as we climbed up the front steps I heard Mr. S running in circles in the front hall, clearly desperate to get outside before he had an accident. "Oh, but I should take the dog out first."

My mom sighed. "Okay, well, that will take a while, so I'll just put on the water."

I felt terrible, but what could I do? Mr. S clearly couldn't wait a second longer. I barely had time to toss my backpack and dance bag inside before snapping on his leash so I could walk him around the block.

I tried to rush so I could help my mom with dinner, but once he was out, Mr. S decided to take his time, sniffing every shrub and mailbox as we went. Just as it looked like we were finally getting back to the house, we ran into the Cronins, out walking their club dogs, Humphrey and Popsicle, after work. It would have been rude not to chat a little. Plus the dogs needed to greet each other. So by the time I got back my mom had dinner well under way, the smell of the marinara sauce she'd gotten out of the freezer and warmed perfuming the whole house.

I took Mr. S's leash off as fast as I could but made sure to hang it on its hook in the hall. My mom was super into keeping things clean, from our home, which sparkled, to our clothes, which never had stains. I did my best to meet her standards, putting my things away, cleaning up after myself, and keeping the downstairs free of clutter the way my mom liked it. Which definitely meant no leash flung over the banister or doorknob.

I headed down the hall to the kitchen and when I walked in I saw that my mom was limping slightly as she took lettuce from the fridge to the counter for salad.

"Did you get hurt at work?" I asked as I went to put on an apron, something I knew she'd appreciate.

"Actually, I tripped over your backpack," she said. "And twisted my ankle."

My shoulders sagged as I remembered throwing it haphazardly into the front hall before taking Mr. S out for his walk. The pack had probably landed right at the bottom of the stairs and my mom, who was rushing since I'd been late, must have fallen right over it. I was messing up everything tonight!

"I'm sorry," I said, feeling awful.

"It's okay," she said in her tired voice that let me know it was not okay but that she had nagged me enough for one day. Which actually felt a lot worse than being nagged.

"I'll be more careful," I promised. "About everything."

And I meant it, I really did.

So after dinner I helped clean up, I emptied my dance clothes into the hamper, and then I started my homework. I finished up math and English and then started my research on Mongolia. No lions but it turned out they had wild horses, which were pretty cool. In fact, I got so into reading about them that my mom had to knock on the door and tell me it was time for bed.

It was only after I'd taken Mr. S for his last walk of the night and then brushed my teeth and settled into bed that I realized I'd forgotten something: calling people from the Dog Club wait list.

3

"See you at the shelter!" Kim called as the four of us parted ways at the intersection of Market and Grove Streets. It was a perfect, brisk fall day, the sun shining on the brilliant red and yellow trees as I waved to my friends and then headed toward Jinx's house. It was time for another meeting of the Roxbury Park Dog Club and we were doing pickups before gathering at the shelter for an afternoon of doggy fun.

My feet crunched through fallen leaves as I turned on Calico Drive and then up the path to Jinx's front door. Jinx was a newer club member, a feisty and fun reddish tan mix whose little face had a pointed snout like a fox. When she heard my footsteps coming up to the porch she ran to the door and barked delightedly.

"Hey, Jinx," I said, locating the house key hidden under a flowerpot and then opening the door. She bounded in excited circles before jumping up and giving me a kiss on the cheek. I bent down and hugged her and was rewarded with another kiss. There was really nothing better than a greeting from a happy dog!

"Let's go see your friends at Dog Club," I told her as I snapped on her leash. "And we're going to get Gus on the way."

Jinx wagged her tail as though she understood every word, and maybe she did. Kim, our resident dog whisperer, always said dogs perceived more than people gave them credit for. And I always felt like Mr. S knew what I was feeling and thinking.

Gus was a brown lab who lived a few blocks away. His owners, the Washingtons, were some of our favorite clients, always supporting the club in any way they could. It was thanks to Mrs. Washington that the Roxbury Park newspaper had featured our club, and sweet Gus was a longtime club member.

When I turned the key in the lock I heard him running down the hall to greet us. Jinx pushed past me to be the first to say hi to her buddy.

"Your house smells yummy," I told Gus as I located his leash in the top drawer in the dresser next to the door. Someone had recently baked an apple pie and the sugary cinnamon scent made my stomach rumble. I decided to ask my mom if we could go apple picking at Montgomery Place, the pick-your-own apple farm outside town, that weekend and bake a pie of our own. But then I remembered my extra dance rehearsals, plus the report I still had to work on, and I realized apple picking would have to wait.

The dogs pranced ahead of me as we headed down

Main Street toward the shelter. I waved to Carmen Lopez, one of the owners of Sugar and Spice, and then heard someone calling me.

I turned and saw Taylor walking with Humphrey, Popsicle, and my very own Mr. S. Taylor wore a pink denim jacket that looked pretty with her brown skin and matched the pink beads in her braids.

"Hey," I called as the dogs and I waited for them to catch up.

Mr. S was nearly blind but he knew my voice and my scent, and his whole body wriggled with joy as I knelt down to snuggle him.

"This guy was sure happy to see me," Taylor said, gesturing to Mr. S and then reaching over to pet Gus and Jinx, who were cheerfully greeting their puppy friends. "He really needed to go out."

"Yeah. Kim said older dogs need to go out more often," I said, scratching Mr. S's soft ears and then standing up so we could get going.

"He's a lucky guy to have you to take such good care

of him," Taylor said as we walked toward the shelter.

I was the lucky one—nothing made me happier than my Mr. S. But I did have to admit the extra walk had made things a bit harder the day before.

"I wish we could get a pet, but my dad says there are enough of us to feed already," Taylor said, rolling her eyes at her dad's silly humor. Taylor's mom had died when Taylor was little but their house was full with Taylor and her three older sisters.

"Maybe when Jasmine and Tasha move out you can talk him into a puppy," I said. Jasmine and Tasha were twins, and since they were juniors in high school they were starting to think about college.

Taylor grinned. "I'm hoping I can wear him down before that."

As we drew close to the shelter, the dogs began moving faster, eager to get inside and start playing. Taylor opened the door and the sound of barking dogs, laughing people, and bouncing balls greeted us. The main room of the shelter was big and open, with a new linoleum floor. There was a small bathroom off to one side, as well as the room where the dog food was stored, though the dogs were usually fed after we left. Alice's office was up front, while bins of toys were stored on the shelves along one side. The wall on the other side was lined with cages that each had a soft doggy bed and blanket. That was where the dogs slept at night, but they were always open during the day, in case a dog wanted to take a nap or spend a little quiet time alone. Out back was a big fenced-in yard where we often took the dogs to play on warm days like today. After all the stress of the past few days I was eager to get out there and run around with the dogs.

"Hi, y'all," Taylor said, her musical Southern accent coming out in full force as we waved to Alice, Caley, and Tim. Caley was throwing a Frisbee for Boxer, our resident boxer, who was deeply attached to the green flying disc. Tim was playing fetch with Daisy, a dachshund whose owner dropped her off for club meetings; Gracie, a cream-colored sweetie of a pup; and Big Al, one of the two newest dogs to arrive at the shelter. Big Al was a tiny tan mix with a terrier-like face. He was scared of everything, so Alice had given him a tough name, to help him be brave. Today as he raced after Daisy and Gracie, it seemed to be working. But when I released Gus and Jinx from their leashes and they ran to join the fun, Big Al darted back to his cage and stared out with a fearful expression.

"Poor guy," Taylor said, walking over to pet him. She'd unleashed Mr. S, Humphrey, and Popsicle, and her camera was slung over one shoulder. Taylor was our official club photographer, while Kim wrote our blog, the Dog Club Diary, which we updated after every meeting so owners would always know what their pups were up to.

"Don't worry, Big Al will get used to things soon enough," Alice said. The head of the shelter wore one of her usual dog T-shirts, this one with three happy dogs and the slogan "Rescue a friend." It was cool the way Alice worked so hard to find homes for dogs.

Though right now she was busy with Violet, the other new arrival at the shelter. And Violet's problem was pretty much the opposite of Big Al's: instead of cowering in fear, Violet went after everything as aggressively as she could. So far there hadn't been any actual fights between the dogs, but that was only because Alice and the rest of us were keeping a close eye on Violet.

"How's Violet been so far today?" Kim asked. I hadn't heard her come in with Missy, who was actually our English teacher's Yorkie, a rescue from a puppy mill who could be a bit skittish. Following behind was Hattie, a sheepdog puppy who was also a former shelter dog happy to come back and play for the afternoon.

Alice sighed. "Well, she tried to steal Boxer's breakfast, which did not go over well, and just now she got snarly with Gracie over a chew toy." She gestured to the rubber hamburger nearby.

Violet, a pretty Dalmatian with long floppy ears and big brown eyes, looked up at us sulkily.

"I've read that Dalmatians can be high-strung,

especially if they don't get enough exercise," Kim said, holding out a hand for Violet to sniff. "We can take her on extra walks and make sure she gets a lot of running in." As always, Kim had a calming effect. Violet touched Kim's hand gently, then butted it with her head to be petted.

"She can be a love when she wants to be," Alice said, smiling down at Violet. "And yes, I think making sure she runs around enough will be good for her."

The door opened again and Bri came in with Waffles and her own Lily. When Bri unclipped their leashes, Lily ran over to say hi to Boxer while Waffles walked over to a tennis ball that was on the floor. He picked it up and carried it to Caley, who obliged him by sending it flying across the room.

"Is there anything else we can do to help Violet?" I asked. I knew Alice would never give up on a dog, even one that was a challenge, but she had to make sure the rest of the dogs were safe and comfortable. And if Violet continued to act out, that could be an issue.

"My mom said Dalmatians need training," Bri said. "And it has to be very specific. Firm but loving."

Alice smiled again. "Your mom came by earlier and told me the very same thing," she said. Although they ran very different dog centers, Bri's mom and Alice had become friends and now tried to work together as much as they could to help dogs in the community. And dog training was Bri's mom's area of expertise, so I knew her advice would be good. "She gave me some pointers that I'm going to try out."

Bri grinned. I knew it had been hard on her when her mom was critical of the club and the shelter, so she was very happy that her mom was an ally to Alice now.

"Should we work on training her too?" Kim asked, still stroking Violet's soft ears.

Alice shook her head. "I think for now her training needs to be limited," she said. "You guys can focus on getting her a good workout when you come. That will help a lot. She'll adjust, it just might take some time."

"Sounds good to me," Kim said. She headed over

to a bin of toys and pulled out a blue rubber ball. When she tossed it, Violet flew after it, Hattie and Lily on her heels.

Oscar, the resident cat who thought he was dog, picked his way daintily around the toys and jumped up to his red cat bed on the windowsill. He looked around for a moment, then began grooming one of his soft gray paws.

The phone in Alice's office rang and she went in to get it.

"Maybe that's someone else wanting to sign up for the club," Taylor said cheerfully. She had slid down to the floor and was cuddling Missy. The small Yorkie would always be skittish because of her time in a puppy mill. But Kim and our teacher, Mrs. Benson, had worked wonders bringing sweet Missy out of her shell and helping her to trust people again. Not so long ago she'd have run from Taylor, but now she leaned against her, panting happily. Moments like this made me so proud to be part of our club that my heart swelled and a big smile took over my face.

But then Bri spoke up. "When are the new dogs coming for their trial visits?" she asked me. She was playing tug-of-war with Popsicle, using her favorite rope bone, but looked up at me expectantly.

My smile disappeared. "Um, I actually didn't have time to call anyone last night," I said, my voice tight. "I was late to dance and then I had to walk Mr. S and help my mom with dinner and then there was the social studies report."

"No problem," Kim said. Her eyes were on Violet, Hattie, and Lily, making sure Violet was behaving, and her words made me feel better.

Bri frowned, though. "We're all busy," she said. "But we can't keep people waiting too long. It will give our club a bad reputation."

Her words made my skin all itchy. I knew about making sure we treated all customers, including potential ones, well. I didn't need her explaining that to me. And she certainly wasn't as busy as I was. Her only job at the club was designing some graphics for the website. But as I opened my mouth to snap back, Taylor spoke up.

"One more day won't make a difference," she said.

Bri nodded immediately. "You're right," she said to Taylor, then looked at me sheepishly. "Sorry if I was talking like my mom the businesswoman for a minute there."

My shoulders, which had hitched up, now relaxed. "No problem," I said. "And you and your mom are both right—we really don't want to keep people waiting. I'll call tonight for sure."

"Great," Bri said as Popsicle gave the rope bone a hearty tug and pulled it out of her hands. "You're so clever," Bri cooed, giving her a kiss before the puppy pranced away to show her prize to her friends.

Tim had a few of the dogs playing with Boxer and the Frisbee and Bri went over to join them. Missy wandered off to find Humphrey, her best buddy, who was napping in a corner. Humphrey was a typical lazy but loving basset hound and he gave a pleased yip when Missy woke him up. Taylor went over to spend more time with Big Al, who was still in his cage, lying down on a cozy fleece blanket. I headed over to Caley, who was throwing a tennis ball for Mr. S, Gus, Daisy, Jinx, and Waffles.

"How's it going?" Caley asked as I picked up a second tennis ball so the dogs could have double the fun. "You're getting ready for a dance recital, right?"

I nodded.

"I know how busy rehearsals can make your life," Caley said sympathetically as she brushed a red curl back from her face. Caley was wearing one of her signature unique outfits, this one a pair of skinny jeans paired with white sneakers she'd drizzled with paint and a vintage gold satin tunic from a thrift shop. She was outrageous and fun, and it was no surprise that she starred in all the high school plays and musicals. Which meant she knew exactly how crazy preparing for a show could be.

"It's tough," I said as I sent the yellow ball zipping across the room, grinning as Mr. S and Gus barreled after it and nearly ran down Boxer as he galloped for the Frisbee. "I mean, it's fun too. I love dancing and this is going to be my first big solo, which is awesome. But it makes it so hard to get anything else done."

"Tell me about it," Caley said, shaking her head as she scooped up the tennis ball Daisy dropped at her feet. At this point both balls were pretty wet but we were pros who just wiped our soggy hands on our jeans and kept on playing. "Freshman year I nearly flunked algebra because I was playing Peter in the fall production of *Peter Pan*."

Yikes, that didn't sound good!

"But I'm better at balancing it all now," she went on. "I wake up early to run lines so I have at least an hour at night for homework. And I see my friends a little less in the weeks right before the show, though most of them are in drama so we hang out at rehearsals anyway."

That was like me with Dog Club—it was the perfect time to see my friends. Though of course I'd still go to our sleepovers. There was no way I'd miss those. "What else do you do?" I asked, hoping for more suggestions. Taylor complained about having three big sisters and Kim griped about her older brother, Matt, but I had always wanted an older sibling to give me advice.

"Well, I get help," Caley said. "My brother takes on my chores when the rehearsals start getting long and I pay him back by doing all of his after the play closes and I have time again," she said.

Since I was an only child that wasn't going to work for me, which was too bad. Help sounded, well, helpful.

There was a commotion in the corner as Daisy tried to take the ball Violet was after and Violet growled. Bri was closest and reached out toward the Dalmatian, whose teeth were bared.

"Careful, don't put your hand near her mouth," Kim said, rushing toward them.

"I wasn't going to," I heard Bri mutter as she stepped aside so that Kim could speak in her low, soothing voice to Violet, who calmed quickly. Kim also patted Daisy, who had been looking at Violet uncertainly but who also settled down under the capable care of our resident dog whisperer.

"Maybe we should take this party outside," Taylor said, looking uncertainly at Kim and Violet.

Kim nodded. "Great idea," she said. "I think Violet could use a good run."

I could too. "I'll be 'it' for doggy tag," I said brightly, eager to get outside and get some exercise for myself as well as the dogs.

"It's on," Tim said as we began herding the dogs toward the back door.

As I began coaxing Big Al out of his cage, hoping he'd be willing to give the great outdoors a try, I heard the phone in Alice's office ring. A moment later she stepped out. "Sasha, it's someone from the club wait list," she said. "They'd like to speak with you."

My shoulders sagged a little as I realized this meant I couldn't go right outside.

"Maybe you can set them up for a visit," Taylor said.

"That way you won't have to call anyone tonight."

Bri turned to me with a frown. "Well, only if that's the person at the top of the wait list," she said. "Otherwise it's not fair."

"Don't worry, I know," I said with a sigh. I had a feeling I knew exactly who was calling and it was not the person on the top of the list. It was a woman named Mrs. Rider, who called a lot, hoping that her dog Maxine could get into the club. It was great that she was so interested, but she tended to show it by talking my ear off, going on and on about Maxine and asking me all kinds of questions about the club hours and policies. A call with her could easily eat up thirty minutes and that was about how long we had to play outside. Which meant no doggy tag for me.

My feet were heavy as I walked toward Alice's office to do my job for the club while everyone else headed out into the yard for an afternoon of fun.

4

"One more time, ladies, and smile," Madame Florence called over the music.

I wiped a hand across my brow, which was literally dripping with sweat, and took a deep breath. My heart was pounding, my leg muscles were screaming, my arms were like rubber bands, and my lungs were scraped raw. In other words, I felt amazing. Nothing was as exhilarating as dance, my body melding with the music, soaring through the steps it had taken me weeks to learn, flying across the studio, light as a feather. It was easy to smile as we lined up for a final run-through of our recital finale.

"I don't know how you do it," my friend Asha whispered as we waited for Madame Florence to give us our cue. Her olive skin was flushed and her short black hair shone with sweat. "I'm ready to collapse."

I grinned at her. "You can't fool me," I said quietly. "I saw how you were leaping like you had wings on."

Asha grinned back. "I guess it's only when the music stops that the wings fall off and I feel how sore I am."

Then it was our turn and we whipped through a series of perfect spins in unison.

"Brava, ladies," Madame Florence said, nodding with approval when the dance was done. "Good work today. Now let's begin our cooldown."

I lined up with the rest of my class but then Madame Florence looked at me. "Sasha, you will stay to practice your solo?"

I nodded reluctantly. I hated the thought of keeping my mom waiting again. But at the same time I knew I needed every second of practice time Madame Florence was willing to offer me.

So while the class stretched out the stress of our intense workout, I ran through the steps on my own. And as my classmates slipped out of the studio, back to the dressing room, I ran through the sequence again, this time under Madame Florence's careful eye.

"Hold your arms a bit higher on the axel turn at the end," she said to me after we'd run through it twice. "But I do think you're getting there."

That was high praise from Madame Florence, so I was beaming under all the sweat as I scurried into the dressing room to grab my stuff. I didn't have time to change, so I just shoved my street clothes into my dance bag, grabbed my backpack, and raced down the stairs to the front of the building where I knew my mom would be waiting in the parking lot, probably tapping her fingers on the steering wheel. Or texting someone from work on her phone.

Except she wasn't doing either of those things, because she wasn't there. The lot was empty, save for Madame Florence's black car off in the far corner. I stood on the bottom step, looking in each direction, but there were no vehicles coming, no sign of my mom. Had she forgotten? That seemed impossible. While I forgot things a lot, my mom never, ever did. Had she waited for me, gotten fed up, and left? I could see her getting annoyed, but not abandoning me on a chilly fall evening two miles from home.

Clearly I needed to call her. I set my stuff down and began rooting around in my backpack for my phone. My mom always told me I needed to put it in the same pocket every time, so it would be easy to find. But while that seemed like good advice, I never remembered to actually do it. And when I finally found my phone, which had gotten wedged inside my binder, the battery had died. I was shivery in the cool air and about to go back inside to ask if I could use Madame Florence's phone when I saw my mom's car turning into the lot.

I practically ran over and pulled open the door. "Is everything okay?" I asked breathlessly. Seeing her there, with her hair perfectly styled, her business suit as crisp as it had been that morning, made me realize how worried I'd been.

"I had that late conference call at work, remember?" she asked, frowning slightly. "I reminded you about it this morning."

"Oh," I said, sinking down on the seat. "I forgot."

I heard my mom sigh quietly and my relief at seeing her was replaced by the heavy feeling of having let her down. "Sorry," I said. "I guess I was just so focused on remembering my dance bag and all my stuff for school that I missed it when you told me."

We were stopped at the light on Main Street and now my mom smiled at me. "I know how busy you are, sweetie," she said. "I just hate for you to worry unnecessarily."

"I'll listen better next time," I said.

But as my mom turned the car down Spring Street and our house came into view, and I thought about walking Mr. S, helping with dinner, and getting at least a little more research done on those Mongolian horses, I was the one sighing.

Because I knew that doing better was a lot easier said than done.

I stayed up late that night working on my report. Normally my mom came to my room to tell me to turn off the light and sleep, but she was under a tight deadline to finish a brief and didn't notice as my bedtime crept past. I'd been happy to get the work done, but now, after pressing snooze on my alarm clock one too many times and racing to walk Mr. S and get dressed in record time, I was not happy at all. It was a gray, gloomy morning, and my whole body felt like I'd slept less than an hour. Plus I hadn't had time for breakfast, so my stomach was grumbling as I ran to meet my friends. I'd grabbed a banana and I couldn't wait to eat it as we walked to school.

"Hey, Sasha," Bri said, smiling brightly. Her hair was in a complicated twist that looked totally sophisticated and made me feel sloppy in my ponytail that was already coming loose. The fact that I was wearing yesterday's jeans, which had been on the floor and thus the easiest thing to put on, did not help.

"Morning," I mumbled, starting to peel my banana as we crossed the street and headed for school. But I must have been gripping the banana too hard because inside it was a soggy, totally inedible pile of mush.

"Do you want some of my lunch?" Bri asked, noticing my face as I dumped the ruined fruit into the trash can on the corner. "I have fried rice and almond cookies."

"Oh, that's okay, thanks," I said, but just then my stomach gave out a loud growl, making my friends giggle. Normally it would have cracked me up too, but today I was too hungry and cranky to laugh.

Bri unzipped her bag and pulled out a small

Tupperware full of cookies.

"Are you sure you don't mind?" I asked. I was so famished I was ready to eat the container too.

"Go ahead," Bri said.

"Thanks." I took out the delicate wafers and pretty much inhaled them. They helped, but I was still hungry.

"My mom and Alice had dinner together last night," Bri said, tucking the empty cookie container back in her bag. Bri carried a messenger bag instead of a backpack like the rest of us, which made her look like one of the eighth-grade girls. The cool ones. "My mom said they talked a lot about Violet and some new ideas for helping her adjust to being at the shelter. Which will also help her when she gets adopted by a family."

"That's great," Kim said. I kind of wanted her to ask why I was in a bad mood but she was too interested in what Bri was saying to notice.

"Yeah, and they also talked about expanding the

foster program," Bri went on, clearly proud to be the one in the know.

"Terrific," Taylor said, sidestepping a puddle on the sidewalk. "That's really important."

I agreed with that—saving dogs from shelters where they could be killed if they weren't adopted out fast enough was a cause we all cared about deeply. But I did worry a bit that it would take Alice away from Dog Club business and now, when things were so busy and Violet was still having issues fitting in, it felt like a hard time for her to be away more.

"It would be wonderful if we could find homes for some of the dogs who've been in the shelter a while, like Boxer and Gracie," Kim said, her feet crunching on a few stray fallen leaves.

"I'd miss Boxer," I said, thinking about our boisterous and loving big guy. "But he'd be so happy to have a family of his own."

"Whoever takes him better have him join the club, though," Taylor said. "That or we'd have to visit him every week." I grinned, remembering back at the very beginning of our time at the shelter when Boxer and the other big dogs had made Taylor nervous. Things had really changed since then. And thinking about that made my mood pick up.

"Opening more spaces at the shelter will be great," Kim said. She'd put her sandy blonde hair back in barrettes today and was fiddling with one of them.

"Speaking of open spaces for dogs, were you able to talk to those families on the club wait list yet?" Bri asked, turning to me expectantly.

I sucked in my breath because yet again I'd forgotten. What with wanting to help my mom, walking Mr. S, and the report, my evening had been crammed. But I couldn't admit it to Bri, with her perfect hair and her cool messenger bag, who always did everything she was supposed to. And who was nowhere near as busy as me.

"I left a message," I said quickly, the lie thorny in my throat. I coughed a little but it didn't help.

"Great," Bri said, nodding.

We stood in silence on the corner for a moment as we waited for the light to change and I squirmed slightly, worried my friends could tell I was lying. I promised myself that I'd call that afternoon to make up for it.

"How's your research going?" Taylor asked Kim, as the Walk sign lit up and we crossed over Bridgeford Drive.

Kim sighed. "Not great," she said. "I've found all these sources to read, but it's hard to figure out what I need to include to give a full sense of Tanzania. I mean, he said write about culture, but what if I choose the wrong parts of the culture?"

Mr. Martin was a very enthusiastic social studies teacher, but sometimes his directions were kind of vague. "Yeah, I have the same problem with mine," I said. "I read all this neat information about wild horses, but I know I need to write about other cultural stuff too."

"I'm going to go to the library this afternoon and

ask Ms. Cho to help me find some books and figure out what to focus on," Kim said. Ms. Cho was the school librarian and always got excited to help students with anything related to books. She was the perfect person to ask for help. "You should come too, Sash, and we can have a study fest."

"Good idea," I said. I had a rare afternoon off and spending it in the library sounded like a great plan.

"What about Mr. S?" Bri asked. "Doesn't he need to be walked right after school?"

I knew she was trying to help, but I couldn't help feeling a twinge of annoyance that she'd found a way to mess up my plans.

"On dance days he has to wait a little longer," I said, feeling guilty but knowing I really needed to get some work done if I wanted to finish this report on time. "I think if I just stay an hour or so in the library he'll be okay."

"I can walk him," Taylor offered. "Your house isn't that far from my photography class. And that way you can stay at the library 'til dinner."

"Are you sure you don't mind?" I asked, relief washing over me at the idea of a few hours to work on my report.

Taylor laughed. "Mind getting a little puppy time with Mr. S? I don't think so."

"Thanks," I said gratefully. "Now I just have to figure out what else to research."

Mrs. Cronin, Humphrey and Popsicle's owner, drove by on her way to work at the bank and waved. "Food is an important part of culture," Bri said as we waved back. "And so is art."

"You're lucky you get to write about pizza and all the famous statues they have in Italy," I said, hearing a slight edge in my voice. "I don't even know what they eat in Mongolia. It's not like there are Mongolian restaurants everywhere, the way there are with Italian restaurants."

"Actually, we lived near a Mongolian restaurant in DC," Bri said. Her family had moved from DC two years ago, and although Bri loved Roxbury Park, I knew there were certain things she really missed about her old hometown. And judging from the look on her face, it seemed like this restaurant was one of them. "They had this special barbecue and it was delicious."

"That sounds tasty," Taylor said, raising an eyebrow. "But I'm not sure it can compete with Southern barbecue."

Bri laughed at that. "They're totally different, don't worry. No one would ever question the deliciousness of Southern cooking."

Taylor ginned. "Glad that's understood."

Bri glanced at me. "Sasha, I can tell you about the menu or we could look it up online. There might even be a Mongolian place in one of the bigger towns around that we could go to some weekend."

I felt bad I'd been snippy when she was being so helpful.

"I'm not sure I have time for that, but it'd be great

if you could help me look up your restaurant online," I said gratefully. "Thanks."

Bri grinned. "The only thing is that it will make us hungry," she said.

And as if on cue my stomach growled again.

This time when my friends laughed, I joined in too.

5

Once again I was late to meet everyone at our lockers before heading out to Dog Club. But this time I had a good reason.

"Sorry," I said, rushing up to my friends, who were grouped around Kim's locker, waiting for me. "I got a text from the Santagelos and I wanted to write back right away."

"Who are the Santagelos?" Kim asked as we walked briskly for the front door of the school. The halls had pretty much emptied out, which meant I was running even later than I'd thought. "And why are they texting you?"

Usually Alice was the go-between with clients unless I was using the shelter phone, since my mom didn't want strangers to have my number.

"The first family from the Dog Club waiting list," I said, shooting a glance at Bri, who smiled. "Alice and I both talked to them and we decided it's okay for them to be in touch with me about scheduling because it's gotten complicated. They're super busy, so we're having trouble finding a time for them to bring their dog Boris in for a visit."

"Boris is a cute name," Taylor said as we headed out into the sunny afternoon. "What kind of dog is he?"

"A Newfoundland," I said, grinning at the thought of one of the big black dogs joining the club. "And he's still a puppy, though he's been trained. Mrs. Santagelo said he's like a big teddy bear."

"Aw," Taylor said, grinning along with me. "He sounds awesome."

"Yeah, I can't wait to meet him," I agreed. "I wish it wasn't so hard to set a time for him to come in, but Mrs. Santagelo is the weekday manager at Old Farm Market and her husband travels most of the time for his job, so they aren't around very much." "Hard" was an understatement: I'd been on the phone most of last night trying to find a time that worked and we had finally agreed on Friday afternoon. But the text I'd just gotten said that her work schedule had changed and we needed to start over. "I also set up an appointment for a second family, the Golds, to bring their dog in," I said. "Her name is Dixie and she's a mix."

"You did a lot of work last night," Taylor said.

I nodded. "Yeah, but it was good to get it done," I said. I decided not to think about how the hours on the phone had made me fall even further behind on my report. The afternoon in the library had shown me how much more work I had to do to finish it. It didn't help that after reading a bunch of menus from Mongolian barbecue restaurants, I'd discovered that it wasn't even Mongolian! It had been invented in Taiwan. I was glad I'd found out, though—Mr. Martin would not be impressed if I wrote about cuisine that wasn't even from Mongolia.

"I'm glad we'll be filling up the club," Bri said. "And getting some of those families off the wait list."

"They were excited," I said, grinning at the memory. "I felt like I was calling to tell them they won the lottery. Mrs. Santagelo actually screamed she was so thrilled."

Taylor grinned. "That's so cool. Those calls must be fun to make."

I nodded but couldn't help thinking that they would be more fun if they didn't take so long.

We paused at the corner as a neighbor who lived down the block, Mrs. Attie, drove by and waved.

"So remind me what we need for our sleepover on Saturday," Bri said. "I want to make sure I get everything right." This was her first time hosting our weekly sleepover and she was clearly excited about it.

"Well, as long as you have my caviar and truffles, you're ready," Taylor said in a snooty British accent that cracked us all up.

"I don't even know what a truffle is," I said.

Taylor shrugged. "Me neither. It just sounds fancy."

"Forget fancy," Kim advised Bri. "We're just happy we get to hang out at your house."

"I want to make sure we have everything we need for the milk shakes, though," Bri said. We had a tradition of creating delectable milk shakes complete with a variety of mix-ins.

"Make sure you get Oreos," Taylor said. "And caramel sauce for Kim. Sasha's favorite is rainbow sprinkles, so definitely don't forget those."

I smiled. The sprinkles added both color and crunch to my milk shakes, and while I liked trying different ice-cream flavors and new mix-ins, my sprinkles were essential.

"Got it," Bri said. "And you'll bring Mr. S, right, Sash? So he and Lily can have a doggy sleepover?"

"Definitely," I agreed. Our pups were really cute all cuddled up together.

"I need to remember to bring my camera for some doggy sleepover shots," Taylor said, smiling.

"That would be awesome," Bri said. "And you guys will finally get to meet my dad because he's actually home this weekend."

"Cool," Taylor said, and Kim and I nodded in agreement.

"He brought back these special dried soybeans so my mom can make us her famous tofu in a clay pot," Bri added proudly.

Normally I think all of us would have wrinkled our noses at the thought of eating tofu, but we'd sampled enough of Bri's mom's cooking in Bri's lunches to know that anything she made was going to be delicious. Plus it was fun to eat authentic Chinese food. I was definitely looking forward to this sleepover.

We scuffed through a pile of leaves that had blown onto the sidewalk, their fresh smell perfuming the air.

"Okay, so I'm getting Waffles and Lily," Kim said, beginning to go through our afternoon pickup schedule. Just then my phone chirped with a text. Sure enough it was from the Santagelos, asking if Monday at six would work. I began typing back, explaining that six was when the club ended and so it wouldn't be good for them to come to the shelter then.

I tried to follow what my friends were saying, but it was hard to text and listen at the same time. And when I nearly tripped on a crack in the sidewalk I realized it was hard to text and walk too. Kim took my arm to help guide me as we walked the last block together.

"See you guys in a few minutes," Taylor called when we'd reached the corner. I waved as my friends headed off to get their dogs, then typed in more dates and times for the Santagelos to consider. We finally found a time that worked—next Wednesday—and I stuffed my phone into my backpack and took off down the street toward Waffles's house. I didn't want to keep him waiting!

But when I climbed the steps there was no sound of dog paws padding up to the door and no bark of greeting when I opened it. The house was empty and Waffles's leash was missing. What was going on?

And that's when I realized my mistake: Kim was the one picking up Waffles and I was supposed to get— actually, I didn't even know who I was supposed to get. This was a disaster!

I fumbled around in my backpack, located my phone, and called Kim. "I went to the wrong house," I wailed the second she answered. "Which dogs am I supposed to get?"

"Missy and Hattie," Kim said right away. "Taylor's getting Jinx and Gus, so she's not that far from the Wongs' house. I can call and ask her to pick up Hattie there, but do you think you can get Missy? I don't think she can handle being walked with three other dogs yet."

"I'm on my way," I said, clicking off my phone and shoving it in my pocket as I took off running toward

Missy's house. I was sweating when I arrived and flew up the steps two at a time. And not the good kind of sweat that came from dance: this was clammy and sticky, making my hair a soggy mess. But I had bigger things to worry about because when I walked into Mrs. Benson's house, there was no sign of Missy. Unlike at Waffles's house, though, her leash was still on the front table in the hall. And I suddenly realized that my race up the steps of the house had scared poor Missy off.

I sighed, unable to believe I'd messed this up too. But I knew the only thing to do now was find Missy, so I began to look around.

It felt weird to wander around my English teacher's house but I didn't really have a choice. I searched for Missy in the living room (where I learned that Mrs. Benson was a very tidy housekeeper and had subscriptions to *National Geographic*, *The New Yorker*, and *ESPN Magazine*, a funny mix). There was no sign of the little dog in the kitchen, which was also sparkling clean, or the dining room. I so didn't want to go into my teacher's bedroom, but luckily I heard a scuffling sound in the back bathroom and finally located Missy, who had stuffed herself behind the sink.

"Hi, sweet Missy," I said gently, squatting down and reaching out my hand for her to sniff.

It took another ten minutes but I managed to coax the skittish Yorkie out of the house. Despite my eagerness to get to the shelter, I let Missy take the lead and she went slowly, sniffing carefully at mailboxes, trees, and shrubs as we made our way into town and arrived at Dog Club at last.

We were over half an hour late, and a game of doggy basketball, Tim's creation that involved a laundry basket, an orange ball, and a lot of running, was in full swing. No one but Mr. S even noticed that Missy and I had shown up. I unleashed her and then bent down to hug Mr. S, who wriggled in delight. He always made me feel better.

I leaned against the wall snuggling Mr. S and watching the game. Bri, whose undefeated streak as a doggy basketball coach was legendary, at least inside these four walls, was cheering on her team of Daisy, Gus, Boxer, and Lily. Tim, the opposing coach, was encouraging Waffles, who had the orange ball in his mouth.

"Go, Waffles, make the basket!" Tim shouted, gesturing furiously to the laundry basket that sat in the middle of the floor.

But Waffles decided that running in circles with the ball and being chased by his friends was more fun and he took off in the opposite direction.

"Take the ball, Hattie," Tim yelled desperately to the small sheepdog who was nearby.

Hattie was a top scorer. She loved dropping the ball into the laundry basket. But Hattie had just spotted Missy and pranced over to say hello. Meanwhile Waffles let go of the ball, Boxer grabbed it, and moments later he scored two points for Bri's team.

"Victory is ours!" Bri shouted, raising her hands over her head and pumping her fists.

Tim slid down to the floor with a groan. "We were

so close," he told Humphrey, who came over and settled on his lap.

"Not really," Bri said breezily. She loved rubbing her wins in Tim's face.

"Hey, Sasha," Taylor said, coming over from where she and Caley had been playing fetch with Popsicle and Jinx. She had out her camera and paused to take a quick shot of Boxer, who had jumped inside the laundry basket to celebrate his win.

Kim, who had been petting Big Al in his cage, popped out when she heard Taylor say my name. "Sash, you made it," she said, coming over to us.

"Yeah, and I'm so sorry I messed up the pickup schedule," I said. I turned to Taylor as Mr. S headed over to play with Gus. "Thanks for getting Hattie."

"It was no big deal," Taylor said.

Her words helped, but I still felt bad. It was the second time in two days she'd had to come to my rescue. I really needed to be more on top of things.

"Sasha, we should set up reminders for you on your

phone," Bri said, as if she'd been reading my mind. "That way you won't forget things so much."

I knew she was just trying to help, but I was getting tired of the way her help seemed more like criticism.

"I just have a lot to do right now," I said, my voice sharper than I'd intended.

"We're all busy," Bri said, her tone just as sharp. "But we have to pull our weight and take care of the dogs."

I knew she was right about me pulling my weight, but I also knew that we weren't all the same amount of busy. No one in the club, least of all Bri, was as swamped as I was.

"Today was no big deal," Taylor said quickly.

"And we know it was just because you had to text that new client," Kim added loyally.

Bri was about to respond when we heard a loud bark followed by a low growl. We whipped around only to see Violet, the orange ball in her mouth, bearing down on Lily. The fur on the back of Lily's neck was standing up and Violet's ears were flat against her head, both signs that the two dogs were not happy with each other at all.

Bri raced over to Lily, but before she could do anything, Kim was there, soothing Violet and resting a comforting hand on Lily's back. Bri reached out to touch Lily too, but Kim stopped her.

"Hang on a second, Bri," Kim said, not taking her eyes off the dogs. "Let me just get her calm before you pet her."

"She's my dog," Bri pointed out, hands on her hips.

"I know," Kim said, sounding puzzled. "I just want to make sure everyone's okay first."

Bri rolled her eyes but stepped away from the dogs. Kim spoke to them in a low voice and after a moment Lily pranced off cheerfully. Violet, clearly soothed, picked up a stray orange ball and Kim threw it for her. The pair began an easy game of fetch, though I saw Kim's eyes dart in Bri's direction.

Bri's expression was stiff as she headed over to throw

a tennis ball for Lily and Boxer. Hattie, Gus, and Mr. S joined them. Taylor was throwing a yellow Frisbee for Jinx, Waffles, and Popsicle, and Missy went over to where Tim was snuggling Humphrey, so I decided to check on Big Al. The small pup had burrowed into the fleece blanket in his cage but gave a happy yip when he saw me.

"Hi, big guy," I said as I sat down next to him and scratched behind his ears.

Everything appeared okay, but I knew it wasn't. Kim was still looking uneasily at Bri, who was clearly ignoring Kim. I could tell by the way Taylor's shoulders were rigid that she felt worried, and I was still bristling from Bri's remarks, as well as feeling guilty about my mistake, which had started everything in the first place. So things weren't fine, not really.

I was about to suggest a game of doggy tag outside. The weather was kind of damp, but running around would probably cheer all of us up. But just then Alice leaned out of her office.

"Sasha, the Golds are calling for you," she said. Today she was wearing the T-shirt with rainbow-colored paw prints across the front.

"Okay," I said, trying not to sigh as I gave Big Al one last pat and stood up.

I knew it would be good to confirm Dixie's trial visit. If both Boris and Dixie worked out, our club would finally be full again and I'd have one less thing to worry about.

But as I headed to the office to spend time on the phone instead of with the dogs yet again, I wasn't feeling relieved.

I was feeling fed up.

6

The next day Kim and I wolfed down our lunches and then headed to the library to get more work done on our reports. Since I'd learned all about what Mongolians *didn't* eat, it was time to learn what they did consume, along with finding out about their culture. I was way behind on my research and eager to do some catching up.

"How are dance rehearsals going?" Kim asked as we walked down the quiet hallway. Today we were both wearing our Roxbury Park Dog Club T-shirts, something that always made me happy. Alice, Tim, and Caley had surprised us with the shirts when the club first began.

"Okay, I think," I said. "We still have some work to do and my solo definitely needs more practice, but we should be ready for the performance." I hoped so, anyway.

"I know you'll be great," Kim said, patting my arm.

Her confidence felt good and with a pang I realized that it had been ages since we'd been alone, just the two of us. I adored Taylor and liked Bri a lot when she wasn't giving me a hard time, but Kim had been my best friend for years. She was the one who comforted me when my parents split up, and I'd been there for her when her dog Sammy died. History like that was important, and as we turned the corner past my locker, I realized how much I wanted to tell her what was on my mind. Because if anyone would understand, it was Kim.

"I'm starting to feel like things at Dog Club aren't really fair," I said, pulling on a curl that had fallen out of my ponytail.

"What do you mean?" Kim asked immediately, her brown eyes shining with concern as she looked at me.

"It's just—I know you work hard on the Dog Club Diary, and Taylor's always taking great pictures for the blog," I said. "And I guess Bri's stuff with the website design takes time too. But with all the calls I have to make, managing all our old clients and scheduling new ones, it seems like I do more work than anyone else."

Kim nodded. "Yeah, I guess that's true," she said. "But now that you have the Golds and the Santagelos scheduled it probably won't be quite so busy."

"Yeah, but there's still the rest of the wait list," I said. "And if one of those dogs isn't the right fit for the club then I'll have to work that out too." I suddenly felt like I was whining, so I stopped talking.

"They both sound like they'll work out, though," Kim said. We reached the library and headed for a table in the back. "I mean, we set up the website and the blog so owners and potential clients can see exactly what we do every meeting. And if they're still interested after seeing that, it's a safe bet they'll be a good fit for the club."

It was true that after a couple of dogs didn't fit in at the shelter, we'd learned to be very clear about what our club did and didn't offer. But it seemed like Kim thought that meant a lot less work for me, and in reality it didn't. I opened my mouth to explain this and then hesitated. We'd reached our table and Kim's eyes were now on Ms. Cho, the librarian. I knew Kim needed every minute we had to get work done, and honestly I did too. So I closed my mouth and let it drop so we could get started on our research.

But I also let it drop because it didn't seem like Kim really understood how unfair my workload was, compared to everyone else's. And maybe she was right—maybe once things settled in with two new club members, the calls and scheduling wouldn't be so hectic all the time.

So as Ms. Cho came over to offer more help, I tried to push down my doubts about the club and focus on Mongolia.

Saturday afternoon I stayed after dance class to practice my solo with Madame Florence. I was feeling good about the rehearsal when I got home, but as I began to pack my overnight bag for the sleepover at Bri's, I could feel exhaustion creeping into my muscles. I looked longingly at my bed: an afternoon nap would have felt amazing. But my friends were expecting me, so I called Mr. S and the two of us headed over to Bri's house.

Bri's mom was there to greet me at the door, along with Lily, who barked joyfully when she realized that Mr. S had come over to play. Bri's mom smiled affectionately as the two dogs ran around the front hall and then took off for the kitchen. "I don't know who's more excited about this sleepover, you girls or the dogs," she said.

I laughed. "I think it might be a tie."

It was great to see her gaze so lovingly at Lily. She'd had her doubts at first about taking in an older shelter dog. But Lily, with her warm brown eyes and sweet manner, had won Bri's mom over, and now she adored their family pet.

"Hey, Sasha," Bri said as she came into the foyer, Kim and Taylor on her heels. Behind them was a man with short black hair and a big smile who I knew must be Mr. Chen.

"I take it you're the other founding member of the Roxbury Park Dog Club," he said in a hearty, dadlike way. For a moment I missed my own dad, who lived in Seattle, and the goofy dad things he always said when I visited.

"Yes, I'm Sasha," I said, holding out my hand.

He shook it firmly. "It's my pleasure to finally meet you," he said. "And now I'm off to be the assistant chef for the feast being prepared in the kitchen."

"Your dad is really nice," I told Bri after her parents had left.

"Thanks," Bri said, her cheeks pink with pleasure. "And here are some slippers for you."

I'd already taken off my shoes, since that was something my mom insisted on at our house, but I was surprised to see Bri holding out a pair of red felt slippers.

"It's a Chinese custom," Bri explained, and I saw that Taylor and Kim were already sporting their own red footwear. "We keep a supply of slippers for guests to wear when they come over. And don't worry, we wash them after every use."

"This is a really good idea," I said, stepping into them. On a cool day it was nice to wear something warm on my feet. "I'm going to tell my mom we should do it too."

"Let's bring your bag up to my room and see what the dogs are up to," Bri said, leading the way through a living room as clean as the one in my house, then up the stairs.

The dogs were waiting for us in Bri's room, playing together with a thick rope toy.

"Too cute," Taylor said, flopping down on Bri's bed, which had a satin comforter in the same shade of aqua as her curtains.

"Totally," Kim said, rubbing her knuckles on Lily's head before settling on the floor by the dogs. I put my bag in the corner next to Kim's and Taylor's and then claimed the beanbag chair. Taylor made room for Bri to sit on the bed next to her.

"So our parents were out late last night," Taylor said to me.

My mom had been out the night before, but she hadn't told me she was with Taylor's dad. "My mom didn't get home until after my bedtime," I said. "I didn't even know who she was out with—she just said someone from work."

"That someone was my dad," Taylor said, taking a moment to fluff her pillow. "I guess they're working on a case together."

That made sense, but I was surprised my mom hadn't said anything about it—she knew I liked to hear

77

about Taylor's family. Though of course maybe she had said something and I'd just missed it, the way I seemed to be missing a lot of things these days.

Bri had moved from the bed to her desk and was searching for something on her computer. "I want to show you guys this new graphic I made for our website," she said.

We crowded behind her and saw that she'd reworked the font and size of the club name. The letters seemed to be three dimensional and she'd managed to get little dog prints running across them. The effect was definitely pretty cool, but I was surprised when Taylor squealed and Kim clapped her hands together as if Bri had figured out a way to end world hunger or something.

"It's incredible," Taylor said.

"I love it," Kim gushed.

"It's nice," I said. Bri glanced at me. "Really nice," I added quickly. "How did you get the paw prints on the letters like that?"

Bri launched into a long description and after a moment I was lost. I had no idea what raster images and PPIs even were, and I was feeling too tired to ask. Kim and Taylor nodded along, though.

"You should take a class in graphic design at the art center where I take my photography classes," Taylor said when Bri was finally done. "They have advanced courses that would be perfect for you, and the teachers they get are really good. They treat you like a professional, not just a kid with a hobby."

Bri's eyes lit up at this suggestion. "That sounds awesome," she gushed. "I'm totally going to ask my parents if I can do it. And then I can design even more stuff for our website."

Kim and Taylor nodded like this was the greatest thing they'd ever heard.

I cleared my throat. "The Santagelos are bringing Boris to the club on Wednesday and I can't wait to meet him," I said. It was true that I was excited to play with a new puppy, but I was also ready to change the subject, and I knew all of them, especially Bri, were eager to get the club full again.

So I was surprised to see the three of them exchange a look.

"Actually," Kim began, not quite meeting my eyes, "we were talking about this before and we're wondering if maybe we should put off the visitation, just for a week or two."

"What?" I asked. My voice came out louder than I'd intended, but I couldn't believe what I was hearing.

"It's just, with Violet having issues getting along with the other dogs, now might not be the best time to bring a new dog to the shelter," Taylor explained, looking at me with a pleading expression. "It's not that we don't want the other dogs, it's just that it might be better to wait."

"You remember what happened with Violet and Lily," Kim reminded me. I saw Bri scowl slightly at her words. "And Violet might have an even bigger problem with a new dog."

"My mom said Dalmatians are high-strung and need structure," Bri added in a tone that was a bit too bossy for my liking. "And so she might find a new dog disruptive."

"You understand, right?" Taylor asked, putting a hand on my arm.

I resisted the urge to snap at all of them and took a deep breath. "Yes, I do," I said. "It makes a lot of sense and of course I want to do what's best for the dogs. I just wish we'd talked about this before I spent a hundred hours scheduling the visits."

Kim opened her mouth, most likely to say something apologetic, but Bri spoke up first. "We would have if we'd thought of it," she said in such an offhand way I could tell she didn't think it was a big deal.

But it was and I was tired of everyone not understanding that.

"You thought of nagging me about calling to set up those visits every minute of the day, though," I said, not caring that I was snapping now.

Kim's eyes widened and Taylor looked panicked. But Bri just sucked in a breath and glared at me. "Sorry for caring about the club and not wanting to neglect new clients," she said in a snotty tone that made my blood boil.

"I care about the club!" I nearly shouted.

Lily and Mr. S stopped playing and looked up at me uncertainly.

Kim put a hand on my arm. "Sash, we all totally appreciate how much work you do for the club." She shot Bri a look before going on. "I'm really sorry I didn't think of this before. It's my fault you had to do all that extra work."

"I'm sorry too," Taylor said quickly. She was tugging on one of her braids. "I've thought a lot about helping Violet get better adjusted at the shelter, but it didn't occur to me until now that one of the best things we could do was hold off bringing in new dogs."

The anger drained out of me. "No, it's not your fault, either of you," I said, sinking back down into the beanbag chair so I could snuggle Mr. S, who had pressed up against my leg. He always knew when I was upset and tried to make me feel better. "I knew Violet was having problems too. I should have thought about how she'd react before I started calling people."

"What's good is that we realized it before we actually brought another dog in," Taylor said, smiling in relief that everything was okay again.

But just like at Dog Club earlier that week, it wasn't okay, not really. I could still feel a hot coal of anger burning in my stomach every time I looked at Bri, whose expression was hard and who clearly didn't feel like she had done anything wrong at all.

"Dinner's ready!" Bri's mom called.

The four of us trooped back downstairs, the dogs following. "We should give them food before we eat," Bri said to me and I nodded.

Kim and Taylor helped Bri's dad bring out what truly did appear to be a feast while Bri and I got out cans of Mighty Meat Mix for our dogs. Lily and Mr. S jumped about in frantic delight as we took turns with the opener and I couldn't help grinning.

Bri was smiling too. "Lily acts like I'm serving her a five-star meal every time I scoop out some of this for her." She held up a spoon heavy with gloppy dog food and we both laughed.

"Mr. S is the same," I said. "And I don't get it because not only is it gross, it's the same thing every single day. But he acts like it's some incredible new delicacy every time."

"I guess that's a good thing, right?" Bri said, trying to set down Lily's bowl. It was hard because Lily was so eager to eat she kept getting in the way. "I mean, better to be happy about the same thing every day than bored by it."

"Good point," I said, managing to get Mr. S's food on the floor for him.

We headed into the dining room, the coal in my stomach cooled by our moment of bonding over our dogs.

The polished wooden table was covered with steaming serving bowls, and as the scents of sesame oil, garlic, and soy sauce hit me, I realized I was famished. Bri's dad was dishing out rice for everyone and Bri's mom smiled when we sat down. "Let me tell you about the food and then you can decide what you want to try. There's eggplant and black bean sauce, stir-fried beef, sesame chicken, broccoli and garlic sauce, spicy potatoes, tofu in a clay pot, and dried string beans."

"Everything sounds fantastic," Taylor said as Mr. Chen began passing the dishes around the table. "I want to try it all."

"Me too," I agreed, spooning some of the potatoes onto my plate. They were cut in thin, crisp strips and smelled delicious.

Soon we all had our plates filled and began to eat. I started with the tofu, which was rich and spicy, better than any tofu I'd ever had.

"This is fantastic," Taylor said. She had started with the chicken.

"I love the potatoes," Kim added. "How do you get them so yummy?"

Bri's mom smiled. "Rice vinegar," she said.

"They remind me of vinegar potato chips," Bri said. She and her parents were using chopsticks and she expertly scooped up a bite of rice along with some string beans.

"Only better," Kim said, helping herself to more. She, Taylor, and I were using forks, but at some point I wanted to ask Bri to teach me how to use chopsticks because they looked neat.

"I usually don't even like broccoli, but this is so good," Taylor raved, spearing another piece. "This is the best sleepover meal ever."

Bri and her parents beamed.

"Thanks," Bri said. "But your dad's fried chicken is pretty spectacular, Taylor. And Kim, the mac and cheese your mom makes is the best I've ever had."

As the three of them went on and on about the great dishes their parents made, I ate my food quietly, feeling like an outsider because my mom usually just ordered pizza for our sleepovers. Everyone always said they liked it, but I noticed no one was mentioning it now. My mom was good at so many things that I didn't expect her to cook four-course meals for me and my friends. But in the face of all the wonderful things everyone else's parents cooked, I felt left out.

As I took another bite, my thoughts went back to the conversation in Bri's room and I realized maybe I'd gotten so upset because Bri, Kim, and Taylor had made the decision about not bringing new dogs into the shelter without me. They could have waited for me before discussing something that was such a big deal, but they hadn't. Whatever the cause, it did not feel good. And suddenly the tofu, which I'd loved when I first tried it, tasted like a wet napkin in my mouth.

I was silent for the rest of the meal and while we helped bring in the dishes after we'd finished. Not that it mattered, because Bri talked enough for all four of us.

We offered to help wash up but Bri's parents shooed

us out of the kitchen, so we headed into the den where we'd planned to spend the rest of the night watching movies. The room was cozy, with a bookcase in one corner, a table to hold snacks and drinks, and a thick tan rug. Pillows were piled next to the sofa, and the walls, like the ones in the living room and dining room, were decorated with scrolls that had Chinese calligraphy and flowers.

"What should we watch?" Kim asked, flopping down on the cushy red sofa set up opposite the big flat-screen TV.

"Maybe we should watch *101 Dalmatians* in honor of Violet," Taylor joked.

The others laughed but I was still feeling annoyed about what had happened, so I didn't join in. Mr. S cuddled against my legs and I sat down on the rug so I could pull him onto my lap. Taylor settled on the sofa next to Kim, Lily at their feet.

"You guys are so cute," Taylor said, taking out her phone and snapping a picture of me and my dog. For that I did smile.

"You should get some doggy sleepover shots of him with Lily," Bri said.

"That would be great," I said. It felt good to agree with something Bri said.

Taylor ran upstairs for her camera while Bri pulled out some toys for the dogs to play with. We had fun throwing them around and posing with the dogs while Taylor captured everything on her camera. I was finally in a good mood when Bri suggested we head back to the kitchen to make our milk shakes.

"We went a little overboard getting ingredients," Bri said as she began pulling ice-cream cartons out of the freezer. "But we wanted to have everything we needed."

"I think you've got that covered," Taylor said admiringly as Bri set six flavors of ice cream on the counter. "The only problem is I'm not sure what kind to have."

"That just means you should mix flavors," Bri said.

Taylor grinned. "I like that solution."

I did too, though clearly we couldn't just mix everything. The salted caramel and mint chocolate chip would be great together, but add in the coconut pineapple and things could get gross fast.

Now Bri was taking sauces out of the cupboard—caramel, fudge, strawberry, and peanut butter—along with packages of Oreos, chocolate-covered almonds, and pretzels.

"We got some fruit too," she said, going over to the fridge and pulling out containers of fresh blueberries and strawberries. "And I think that's everything. I'll get the mixer and we can get started."

My friends were so busy selecting flavors and add-ins that they didn't see what was missing. But then Kim's brow creased. "Um, Bri, did you get the rainbow sprinkles for Sasha?"

Bri's eyes widened and she nearly dropped the handheld mixer. "Oh no," she moaned. "I forgot. Sasha, I'm so sorry."

"It's okay," I said. Because what else could I say? She and her mom had gotten everything under the sun to make these milk shakes as special as possible. "This is all great. I don't need the sprinkles every time."

"You can branch out and learn new delights," Taylor added in a perfect imitation of Mr. Martin.

We all laughed at that, but mine sounded loud and fake in my ears. I pasted a smile on my face as I scooped ice cream into the big glass Bri handed me because I knew I was being ridiculous: the sprinkles really weren't that big of a deal. And yet, the one thing she forgot to get was the one thing that mattered to me the most.

And that needled at me for the rest of the night.

7

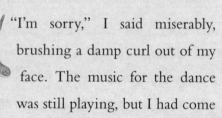

"I'm sorry," I said miserably, brushing a damp curl out of my face. The music for the dance was still playing, but I had come to a screeching halt after messing up a series of barrel turns, a pretty basic jazz step that I should have been able to do in my sleep.

Madame Florence's lips were pursed, but she nodded to acknowledge my apology. I had stayed after dance for more rehearsal time, but it wasn't going well. At all.

And I knew why: ever since Saturday night when the girls had decided not to include me in their discussion about new dogs at the club, my thoughts had been stuck on a hamster wheel, unable to let it go. It wasn't just that they'd left me out: it was the way none of them cared, *really* cared, that so much of my time had been wasted for nothing. I'd tried to explain it to Kim before the sleepover, that I did more work for the club than anyone else. But she hadn't gotten it then and still didn't seem to get it now. The fact that I had the most work was bad enough, but the fact that no one except me even realized it made it worse. And those thoughts spinning around and around my mind had made it impossible to get any research done on Sunday, made me distracted in school, and were distracting me now. Just when I was supposed to be flying through my solo, I was grounded, my body heavy and slow, like a walrus instead of the seagull I needed to be to get all the steps right.

"Let's stop for today," Madame Florence said. "Get some rest, review the routine at home, and we will try again after your next class."

"Okay. And I'm really sorry," I said, feeling awful as I dragged myself back to the dressing room. Now I'd wasted my teacher's time, not to mention my mom's. And mine. The last thing I needed was to spend thirty minutes being bad at my dance.

My mom knew I'd be late leaving the studio but she still looked impatient when I got into the car a few minutes later. I'd barely fastened my seat belt before she was pulling out of the lot.

"How much longer will these extra rehearsals go on?" she asked, a slight frown on her face.

"I think until the show," I said. "But that's in a couple weeks, so not too much longer. Sorry."

My mom glanced at me and smiled. "I'm proud you're working so hard," she said. "And I know you need the extra time since you have a solo. It's just tough getting home so much later."

"I know," I said, sinking down a bit in my seat.

My mom reached over and patted my arm. "It's

worth it to be raising such a skilled dancer," she said affectionately.

I gulped, glad she hadn't seen what a mess I'd made of my dance just now. I had definitely not felt skilled.

Mr. S raced up the moment we walked in the front door, happy to see us and ready for his walk. "I'm just going to take him out and then I'll be back to help with dinner," I told my mom, reaching for Mr. S's leash. Which was not on the hook where it was supposed to be. Where had I put it after I walked him this morning? I looked on the chair, the banister, and the dresser before finally getting down on my hands and knees to look on the floor. It had fallen behind the dresser and poor Mr. S was pawing at the door by the time I had it.

"Sorry, sweet boy," I told Mr. S as we hustled outside. He looked up and gave a small bark, forgiving as always. But as he stopped to sniff the Cronins' mailbox, I felt that hot coal of anger in the pit of my belly again. And this time I wasn't just feeling angry with Bri: I was angry at Taylor and Kim too. Because if I wasn't so busy with Dog Club clients, I'd be done with my report, on top of my dance, and able to do things like help my mom with dinner and walk my dog on time. And every other word out of my mouth wouldn't be "sorry."

I knew it was my fault I wasn't organized. But how could I even start to organize myself when I had this much to do and no one helping me with any of it?

I hurried Mr. S back into the house where my mom was banging dishes around trying to get a salad made and a frozen lasagna heated up and on the table. I set out plates and silverware—after taking off my sneakers, of course—and we finally sat down to eat.

As I took my first bite of the creamy cheese, soft noodle, and gently spiced sauce, I suddenly realized how hungry I was. Apparently dancing badly gave me even more of an appetite than dancing well!

Clearly my mom was hungry too because we both nearly finished our first servings before she asked me about my day.

"I did well on our math test," I said, remembering

that brief moment of pleasure when I'd gotten my paper back today. Of course I'd taken the test almost two weeks ago, before things got crazy busy. Our math teacher was slow to correct and return our work. But I was still pleased with my score and from my mom's smile I could tell she felt the same.

"How are your other classes going?" she asked, taking second helpings of both salad and lasagna.

"Pretty good," I said quickly. I was sure I'd bombed my most recent English quiz and obviously social studies wasn't going well. But until I had actual grades to report, it didn't seem worth getting into. Which meant it was time for a new topic of conversation. "I didn't know you and Taylor's dad were working on a case together," I remarked, remembering what Taylor had said about it a few days ago. I leaned forward to cut myself another piece of lasagna.

My mom shook her head. "We're not," she said, her eyes on my food as I tried to get the lasagna from the pan to my plate. A thousand strands of cheese stretched between the two points. My mom reached over and deftly sliced them so they wouldn't drip all over the table.

"Thanks," I said. "But I thought you had a business dinner with him last Friday, to talk about a case or something."

My mom's cheeks turned pink, maybe from the bite of lasagna she'd just taken: it was hot. "Oh, right, of course," she said quickly. "We were just talking about billing."

I wasn't sure why two lawyers at a firm would need to discuss billing—wasn't that what an accountant did? But then again, it wasn't the first thing I didn't understand about my mom's job. I knew that her work helped protect the environment, but she lost me whenever she started talking about injunctions or the different types of briefs she drafted—and I wasn't even really sure what a brief was.

I helped clean up after we'd finished and then headed upstairs: it was time to stop thinking about Dog

Club and get some serious work done on my report.

But the second I settled into my desk chair, about to open the first book from my pile of books about Mongolia, my phone beeped with a text. I debated even checking it, but what if it was something important? So I swiped past the screensaver, which was a picture of all four of us at the shelter, dogs piled on our laps, and saw that it was from Mrs. Santagelo, confirming that she'd be at the shelter tomorrow.

Yikes! I was sure I'd texted her about the change in plans. I scrolled through my phone and groaned out loud when I saw my mistake: I'd typed out the text but somehow sent it to my drafts folder instead of to the Santagelos. I wrote a response to Mrs. Santagelo, explaining the change and apologizing. Then I checked to see if I'd remembered to cancel with the Golds. While I was doing that, I got an email with the messages that had come in to the Dog Club website—three potential clients who would require responses. I was about to start in on those, but then I heard back from Mrs.

Santagelo, who was understandably annoyed with me. She even asked if our club was always this disorganized! I'd be in trouble with Bri if she ever saw that. This was so not the way to get good word of mouth for our club!

I wrote out a heartfelt apology to Mrs. Santagelo, then responded to all three messages from potential clients. At least I had remembered to text the Golds over the weekend, so that was one less thing to do.

But half an hour later, when I was finally able to start work on my report, I heard Mr. S whine softly—he needed to go out. And when I looked at the clock, I saw why: hours had passed since I had last taken him and it was getting close to my bedtime.

I was blinking back tears as I headed downstairs to walk my dog. The way things were going, I was going to fail this report!

8

The next morning was crisp and sunny and for the first time in ages I was actually on time to meet everyone at the corner for our walk to school.

"Sash, you're here," Taylor said when she saw me. A gust of wind caught her braids and she smiled as she brushed them back from her face.

"Are we late?" Bri asked, pulling her phone out of her pocket in mock concern, making all of us laugh.

"I know, I'm on time, it's a shock," I joked as I

shifted the weight of my backpack. All those library books made it heavy.

"We're happy to see you," Kim said. Her cheeks were pink from the wind as she smiled at me.

"I decided to stop eating breakfast at home," I confessed as we started toward school. I'd realized that eating on the run would tackle two problems at once: being on time in the morning and taking care of my breakfast dishes. So today I had an English muffin wrapped in a paper towel that I held up to show my friends and then bit into.

"Way to multitask," Taylor said.

"I didn't want to be late because I have an invitation for you guys," I said once I'd swallowed.

"Yes," Taylor said immediately. "I'm in."

I laughed. "I haven't even told you what it's for yet."

"If you're there, we're there," Taylor said. Then she made a face of mock concern. "That is, unless you're finally getting around to cleaning out your closet. If that's the case I might be busy after all."

Bri and Kim both laughed at that and I couldn't help joining in. My mom demanded a clean room and I often accomplished this by stuffing things in my closet, stowing them behind boxes and hanging clothes. Taylor joked that one day the whole thing would erupt like a volcano and she was probably right.

"No closet cleaning," I assured them. Taylor drew an arm over her forehead in joking relief. "I was actually wondering if you guys could come for a sleepover after my dance recital next Saturday."

The show was a matinee and I'd already gotten tickets for my friends. No matter how crabby I felt about the last sleepover or the unfair way club jobs were divided, it meant a lot that they would be there. After all, Kim had been coming to see me dance since my very first performance, when I was one of the snowflakes in *The Nutcracker.* I was onstage for all of two minutes, but Kim still brought me a big bouquet of pink roses because she knew they were my favorite. She'd been at every show since, roses in hand, and at this point I couldn't imagine dancing without her there. And having Bri and Taylor with her would be even better.

"A sleepover after your show sounds great," Kim said as Taylor and Bri nodded. "We'll be there."

"My mom and I will make something really special for dinner," I added. My mom and I had not actually discussed this yet—she was so annoyed with me lately that it didn't seem like the best time to ask for a favor. But I figured if I searched out a recipe and wrote down the grocery list and presented it as a fun mother-daughter activity, she couldn't say no. I wasn't sure when we'd actually have time to prepare a meal, but I'd figure that part out later.

"It'll be fun knowing we're invited to the home of the star after the big dance," Kim said proudly.

I squeezed her arm. She was the best!

"What happened to you last night?" Bri asked as she fussed with the combs that held her hair back from her face. "We had a group text about the club meeting today."

"Oh, I didn't even see it," I said. I was done with my muffin and tossed the balled-up paper towel into a garbage can as we passed it. I could feel the muffin bouncing in my stomach with each step—maybe eating on the go wasn't such a great idea after all. "I was so busy writing to the Santagelos and responding to new requests, I didn't check for new texts."

The minute the words were out I knew I'd made a mistake. Taylor's brows scrunched up. Kim bit her lip and Bri put her hands on her hips.

"Wait, aren't the Santagelos the family that was supposed to come into the shelter today, the one we decided to reschedule?" Bri asked sharply.

"Yeah, but it's fine," I said, the words rushed. I so did not want to talk about this.

But of course Bri did. "We made that decision on Saturday," Bri said. "You had days to let them know we needed to change their appointment."

I bristled at her mention of Saturday. "We" hadn't decided; they had.

"Letting people know something like that so last-minute is really unprofessional," Bri went on, shaking her head.

"I did my best," I said between clenched teeth. I did not want to get into this now, right before school.

"The important thing is that they know now, though," Taylor said, her forehead crinkled as she glanced between me and Bri.

Bri looked away.

I hoped Kim would say something supportive, but she was twisting a lock of hair and acting like she hadn't even heard Bri's last remark. "Are you guys ready for the math test?" she asked.

The English muffin was a rock in my belly. I'd completely forgotten about the test.

"You'll do great," Taylor said comfortingly to Kim.

"Anna helped me a lot," Kim said, smiling slightly. "I think I'm ready."

Kim had a tutor—of course she was ready. The only

one poised to fail the test, the report, and possibly all of seventh grade, was me.

The wind had picked up by the time the final bell rang.

"It's like a hurricane out here," Bri said, holding up both hands to keep her hair from blowing free of its combs.

"Actually, it's not," Taylor said, with a rare frown. "I used to live in hurricane country and those storms are serious."

"Sorry," Bri muttered, but I could tell she wasn't.

I could sympathize: she'd just been joking and Taylor had kind of overreacted. But since I was annoyed with Bri, I wasn't going to feel bad for her.

"I'm just glad the math test is over," Kim said, obviously eager to change the subject. She'd already told us at lunch that she'd known how to answer every question and was pretty sure she'd aced the exam. So remembering it made her smile, but it gave me an icy feeling. Because unlike Kim, I'd really struggled and had probably gotten my worst grade of the year, at least until I handed in a blank sheet of paper for my Mongolia report.

"Sasha, you remember you're picking up Waffles and Lily today, right?" Bri asked in a bossy tone.

That did nothing to make me feel better. "Of course I do," I snapped.

Bri raised her eyebrows. "You don't need to take my head off about it," she sniffed. "I just figured a reminder wouldn't hurt."

She always figured that.

We'd reached the corner where we had to separate to get our dogs. "See you guys at the shelter," I said, trying to sound cheerful.

I went to get Waffles first and made the unfortunate discovery that he had thrown up right in the front hall. It didn't seem fair to leave that for his owners to find when they came home, so I took a few minutes to clean up before securing Waffles onto his leash and heading to pick up Lily.

Being at Bri's house reminded me of the sleepover that past weekend and it was not a happy memory. "Let's go, Lily," I told the shaggy tan dog, who would not drop the rubber dog bone she held in her mouth. "Put down your toy so we can go see your friends."

Lily looked up at me with sweet brown eyes but kept the toy tight between her teeth. It was impossible to be annoyed with an animal this cute, though, so instead of telling her again to drop the toy, I sat on the floor and hugged her. Waffles climbed right onto my lap next to her. Despite being slightly smooshed it was the best I'd felt all day. I was smiling by the time Lily finally dropped the bone and we were able to head to the shelter.

"Is everything okay?" Bri asked the second the dogs and I walked in. She rushed over and threw her arms around Lily.

"Yeah, it's fine," I said, slightly confused.

"You took so long to get here," Bri said, her voice muffled by Lily's fur. "And you didn't answer my texts.

I was worried something had happened."

"I guess I forgot to turn my phone back on after school," I said, letting Waffles off his leash so he could go play. "Sorry you were worried. It just took a while because Waffles puked and I wanted to clean it up."

"Gross," Taylor said, wrinkling her nose. She was petting Oscar in his cat bed on the windowsill and had overheard me.

"It's nice you cleaned up, though," Bri said, standing up as Lily padded off to greet Boxer, Hattie, and Gus, who were playing with Caley. Big Al, who had been slightly less fearful lately, wandered over and she bent down and rubbed his ears.

For the first time in a while I smiled at Bri and really meant it. Her concern for Lily was sweet and it was nice to hear her say something complimentary about me for once.

I looked around to see who needed an extra hand and was about to join Tim, Jinx, Popsicle, Waffles, and Mr. S, who were playing with a red and orange striped ball, when there came a low growl from the back corner. We all turned to see Violet baring her teeth at Missy, who had accidently walked too close to Violet's cage. Apparently Violet was feeling territorial and Missy, who did not react well to stress, had frozen. Violet took this as a threat and growled again.

Bri was closest and she walked over, beginning to speak to Violet in a soothing voice. Kim was on her heels and carefully scooped up Missy before stepping in front of Bri to pacify Violet. And a moment later, Violet was allowing Kim to rub her ears.

Crisis averted, thanks to our resident dog whisperer.

"Good job, Kim," Alice said. She had come out of her office when the growling began.

I heard Bri snort as she walked past me, her expression stiff.

"Violet's still having a hard time," Alice went on, walking over to stroke the Dalmatian. Violet leaned her head against Alice's leg. "But I'm seeing some improvement."

"I think in this case she just misunderstood Missy's intentions," Kim said. She still held the small Yorkie, who had burrowed against her shoulder.

"And the way Missy froze up just made it worse," Alice agreed. "But I do think we're getting closer and—"

Just then the phone rang and Alice headed back to her office. Since everything had settled down, I decided to join in the game Tim still had going on at the front of the shelter. But the moment I picked up the ball, Alice stuck her head back out of the doorway. "Sasha, it's someone interested in the club," she called.

I looked around to see if the other girls noticed that I was going to have to leave dog playtime to answer the phone yet again. But Kim was coaxing Missy to play with Humphrey, Taylor had started playing fetch with Gracie and Popsicle, and Bri had joined Caley with Hattie, Gus, and Boxer. They didn't even glance up as I sighed and walked into the office. They were too busy having fun.

The call was short but another one came in a few minutes later, and by the time owners began arriving for club pickup a couple of hours later, I'd spent more time in the office on the phone than out playing with the dogs. Again.

Mrs. Washington came in first and Gus bounded up, happy to see her. A minute later Mr. Wong came in for Hattie, with Mr. Cronin right behind him. Mrs. Benson was the last to arrive and as always it was strange to see our English teacher, who usually wore pressed pants and neat button-down shirts, walk through the door in worn jeans and her Ohio State sweatshirt.

"How did things go today?" she asked as Missy walked up and sat on her foot. I couldn't help smiling at how cute Missy was or at Mrs. Benson, who was really just another happy dog owner hugging her pup.

Bri opened her mouth to respond, but Mrs. Benson had already turned to Kim. "Did you make any progress getting her to fetch?"

The two of them launched into a conversation

about Missy while Taylor, Tim, and Caley packed up most of the toys, leaving some out for the shelter dogs. Bri was leashing up Lily and I noticed she was frowning again.

I knew I needed to get my stuff and get Mr. S ready to go, but I'd had so little dog time that I couldn't resist picking up Boxer's Frisbee and tossing it across the room for him. And when he brought it back there was no way I'd deny him a second throw, not when he looked up at me with pleading eyes, eager to race after it again.

"Sasha, we're ready," Bri said in a crabby tone a minute later. Or maybe it was a few minutes. Gracie and Violet had joined the Frisbee game and it had been going so well I didn't want to stop. But Bri, Kim, and Taylor all had their jackets on, and Caley and Tim must have left when I wasn't looking.

"Sorry," I said, stumbling a little as I rushed to get Mr. S leashed up and put on my coat. "I'm ready now," I said, leading the way out.

"Except for your backpack," Bri said drily.

"Whoops," I said sheepishly, going back for it.

We waved good-bye to Alice and walked into the chilly evening. It was dark outside and the streetlights cast a soft glow on the sidewalk as we started down Main Street.

"Now I'm running late," Bri said as she tugged on Lily's leash. Her free hand was jammed in the pocket of her light down jacket and she didn't seem to have noticed that her hair was slipping out of its combs.

"Sorry," I said, my voice pinched because I wasn't actually sorry at all. Mr. S looked up at me, concerned.

"It's bad enough you keep us waiting in the mornings," Bri snapped. "It's not fair to make us late at night too."

"I wasn't late this morning," I pointed out.

"For the first time in ages," Bri grumbled.

Kim and Taylor exchanged a look but neither of them spoke up to defend me.

"I just wanted to stay a little later at Dog Club

because I barely had any time to play with the dogs," I said, the hot coal of anger heating up in my belly. "You probably didn't notice but I was on the phone half the time talking to new clients."

"I hope you didn't mess up scheduling with them too," Bri said snidely. She sounded like her old self, the Bri who said whatever she wanted without thinking about how it might make someone feel.

And how it made me feel was furious. But Kim spoke up before I could say anything.

"Bri, that's not fair," Kim said, clearly upset. "Sasha does a lot for the club."

"So she's always telling us," Bri said, spinning on her heel and nearly getting tangled in Lily's leash so she could face Kim. "And you work your magic with the dogs and Taylor takes pictures—you're all clearly the most important parts of this club."

Kim took a step back, obviously surprised at Bri's attitude. "We're all important to the club," she said uncertainly.

"Actually, Bri has a point," I said, my anger bub-
bling over. "She *doesn't* do as much as the rest of us. And
none of you do as much as I do." Mr. S was looking
from me to Bri, clearly upset. I rubbed his head, which
usually soothed me as well, but not today. I was too
riled up for anything to soothe me now.

"Yeah, we know," Bri said, rolling her eyes. "It's all
you ever talk about." Lily gave a short bark and Bri patted her on the back.

"Because I'm sick of it!" I exploded. "I don't get to
play with the dogs, I'm behind on all my schoolwork,
I messed up at my dance rehearsal, and I'm probably
going to fail our social studies report."

"It's no one else's fault that you're disorganized," Bri
said dismissively.

"Well, it's also no one else's fault that you don't do
more to help out," I said, hands on my hips.

"Actually, that *is* someone else's fault," Bri said tartly
as she rested her gaze on Kim. "Kim takes over everything. She's the *dog whisperer*"—her voice turned sour

on the words—"and she acts like the rest of us don't know anything."

"That's not true," Kim said, her eyes narrowing.

"Yes it is," Bri retorted. "You never let anyone near Violet when there's a problem. You just rush in and take over, like you're the only one who can help."

"This club wouldn't even exist without me," Kim said, biting off the words. "So you're right, I do think I know what I'm doing! And so does Alice and so do all our clients."

"That's because you never give the rest of us a chance," Bri huffed.

"If you want to participate more, just do it," Kim said, tugging viciously at the strap on her backpack.

"You could start by helping me call people back," I said, still indignant about her earlier remarks. "Then you'll see how much time it takes."

"I'd probably get it done in five minutes," Bri said frostily. "And I wouldn't make scheduling mistakes."

"Guys!" Taylor said, holding up a hand like she was

a crossing guard. "Let's calm down. I'm sure we can figure this out."

"Tell *her* to calm down," I said, seething as I glared at Bri.

"Sash, I know you're upset, but you do forget things sometimes. Maybe if you made a list or something, you could get the calls done faster," Taylor said in a way that she clearly meant to be mollifying but that only enraged me more.

"So you think it's my fault, too?" I shouted. Mr. S tipped his head up to look at me, worried that I was so mad. I scratched him behind his ears to help him settle, but my stomach was still churning with anger.

"I was just saying that maybe organizing a bit more would be a good idea," Taylor said meekly, looking at Kim to back her up.

But Kim had folded her arms over her chest. "I can't help with that," she said brusquely. "You guys know how much time I spend on schoolwork and tutoring. I can't be calling people about the wait list or helping you figure out how to manage it, Sasha."

My eyes widened at her words. I couldn't believe Kim would stab me in the back like that! And she wasn't the only one with school problems—thanks to all my Dog Club work, I was drowning in them.

"Right, of course Kim could never be on the *phone* during club because she's the only one who can manage the dogs," Bri said sarcastically. Lily whined and leaned against Bri's leg, obviously upset, but Bri stayed rigid, her eyes flashing.

"Can we all just take a deep breath and discuss this quietly?" Taylor asked, obviously trying to sound diplomatic.

Bri glared. "Okay, let's talk," she said. "What do you think, Taylor? Does Kim boss us around too much or not? And are you as tired of Sasha complaining as the rest of us?"

Taylor gulped. "Um, I really don't want to take sides," she said.

Bri threw up her hands. "Great," she said.

"No, it's just, I think it would be more useful if you guys settled down and tried to listen to each other," Taylor said. Maybe she was trying to be nice, but it came out like she was being condescending.

Kim rolled her eyes. "That's not going to help anything. I already hear Bri loud and clear."

"And we've all heard Sasha complain endlessly and that's just making things worse," Bri snapped. "Maybe if she stopped whining we could—"

"Who are you to tell me what to do?" I interrupted, so angry my hands had balled into fists, Mr. S's leash cutting into my palm.

"Right, I forgot, telling everyone what to do is Kim's job, not mine," Bri said. "Because I don't have a real club job."

"I don't have to listen to this," Kim fumed. She glanced at me, as if waiting to see if I'd defend her. But after her backstabbing comment earlier, there was no way I was speaking up for her. Or Taylor. And certainly not Bri. I was done with all of them.

So I whirled around, tugged Mr. S's leash, and stalked toward home. A small part of me hoped that my friends would call me back, would finally say that they'd realized I was right.

But all I heard behind me was each of my friends stomping off alone.

9

When I got home all I could do was fume. How dare Bri attack me like that! And Kim was such a backstabber. Even Taylor was making me crazy with her refusal to take sides. The whole situation was utterly maddening and I was fed up with all of them.

After a dinner with my mom where I could barely choke down my food, and an hour of trying to focus on my report, it was time to take Mr. S for his walk. I leashed him up and we headed out. The night was cool and there was a gloomy heaviness in the air, like it was going to rain soon. Which matched my mood perfectly.

I let Mr. S lead me down the block, stopping when he wanted to sniff but not really caring where we went or how fast we walked. My head was too full of thoughts about the fight. I was still enraged by Bri and Kim, but I had started to simmer down about Taylor. Yes, it had been annoying to have her act like some kind of adult, telling us to be calm, but maybe if I talked to her one-on-one, without interruptions, she'd see what I was saying. I *was* the one who was right, after all.

So when Mr. S and I got back, I called her.

"Hey," she said eagerly, after picking up right away. "That was crazy after club today."

"I know," I agreed. I was about to say more when she went on.

"Everyone got so worked up, and when you think about it, none of it is that big a deal," she said.

"I'm not so sure," I said slowly. "I mean, I really do

have more work than anyone else in the club and it's not fair."

There was a silence that felt heavier than the night air had been.

"I mean, it's obvious, right?" I asked, a pleading note creeping into my voice.

Taylor cleared her throat and when she spoke her words were stiff. "I really don't think I should take sides," she said.

"It's not taking sides, it's just agreeing with something that's true," I said.

"Maybe we should talk tomorrow when everyone's cooled off," Taylor said.

I was feeling anything but cool. "You have to have an opinion about *something*," I said sharply.

"I don't think it will fix anything to have me get involved," Taylor said, and now she was the one sounding sharp.

"Fine," I snapped, then ended the call before she could say another word. If she was too scared to weigh in, we didn't have anything else to talk about.

I was furious with all three of them for the rest of the night.

The rain beat down on my umbrella and the tops of my rain boots as I walked to school the next day. I glanced at our usual meeting place, just to see if one of my friends might be waiting for me, finally come to her senses and ready to say sorry.

But the only thing on the corner was a big puddle.

As I headed into the building a few minutes later I suddenly wondered if maybe the three of them had made up. What if they had talked without me last night or this morning, the way they'd talked without me about waiting to bring new dogs into the club? The thought brought the tornado rushing back into my stomach.

But when I walked into homeroom I saw that Kim had turned in her seat so that her back was to Taylor. Bri, who sat up in front, was staring at the whiteboard at the front of the room as though it was the most fascinating thing she'd ever seen. So I breathed a sigh of relief as I slid into my own seat, careful not to glance at either Kim or Taylor. I certainly didn't want anyone to think I took back anything I'd said. I mean, I did kind of regret hanging up on Taylor. A little. And not backing Kim when Bri attacked her. But what they'd done to me was worse, so I was not going to be the one to apologize first. That was on them.

As the morning went on I discovered that it was kind of lonely walking through the halls by myself. I'd never thought about it, but I was always with one of my friends, if not all of them, joking and talking as we went from one class to the next. Being alone made my chest feel hollowed out.

But that still didn't mean I was going to say sorry. At lunch I went to the cafeteria and grabbed an energy bar and a yogurt smoothie, which I wolfed down right after I paid for them. I didn't want to sit in the cafeteria because who would I sit with? When I glanced at our table, I saw that it was empty. Bri was sitting with the girls she'd done our last social studies project with and Taylor was at a table with a group of kids who were into art. They were probably talking about photography. I bit my lip at the sight of her laughing with them but then headed out. It was better that I wasn't going to waste time talking in the cafeteria, anyway, because I had better things to do: it was time to get some serious research done on Mongolia.

"Hi, Sasha," Ms. Cho said, smiling from her perch at the circulation desk when I walked into the library, my steps quiet on the thick carpet. "Your partner in crime is waiting for you. Let me know if I can help either of you out with anything." She gestured cheerfully toward the back of the library, where Kim was sitting at our usual table, a stack of books about Tanzania next to her.

"Thanks," I said to Ms. Cho, not sure what to do. I walked slowly toward the back of the library—that was where the research books on different countries were, after all. But I didn't want Kim to think I planned to sit with her. Or did I? I had no idea how to be mad at one of my favorite people in the world, and as I looked at her absently pulling on a lock of hair as she took notes, a wave of remorse washed over me.

But just then Kim looked up, saw me, and scowled. She pushed her pile of Tanzania books into the spot where I usually sat, gave me a defiant look, and went back to work, her mouth a thin line.

My face was on fire as I stalked over to the book-shelf. How could I have felt bad about yesterday for even one second? I certainly hoped she knew I hadn't been planning to sit with her. I'd have told her that much, but I wasn't speaking to her, not ever. Or at least not until she apologized.

I took three books from the shelf and flounced over to the table across from Kim. I made a big show of sitting with my back to her as I opened my notebook and began copying random facts about Mongolia. It was too hard to concentrate when I was this busy snubbing Kim.

It turned out it took a lot of energy to ignore my best friend, even if she did completely deserve it.

"Nice job on your solo today," Dana said as we stood in line for the drinking fountain at the end of rehearsal.

"Thanks," I said, grinning. After an exhausting day of pretending my closest friends were invisible, it had been wonderful to throw myself into dancing. I'd been worried that it would be hard to concentrate again, but it turned out that complicated steps and jazz music were just what I needed. My solo had gone so well that Madame Florence said I didn't need to stay late to practice. "I think we're all looking good."

"Agreed," Dana said. "Madame Florence pushes us so hard some days I just want to quit. But when it all comes together like this, it's worth it."

"Totally," Asha said as she came up to stand behind me. She was still breathing hard from our last dance, which had a lot of spins at the end. "Our show is going to be amazing."

"Kim and Taylor and Bri will be there, right?" Dana asked. The hair that had fallen out of her bun was damp with sweat.

"Um, yeah," I said, reaching down to adjust my jazz shoe. The heaviness of the fight, which had lifted off me during practice, settled back down on my shoulders.

"They're going to be so impressed," Dana said.

"Yeah, you nailed that solo," Asha agreed. "Even your best friends are going to be wanting your autograph."

If they were even talking to me then. It was my turn at the fountain and as I bent over and took a long sip of water, I couldn't help thinking about all my plans for a fabulous sleepover after my performance. Sure, there were other things I could do to celebrate. But honestly, I knew there was nothing I wanted more than to be with my best friends. I hated to admit it, but I missed all of them, even Bri.

But I wasn't sure that meant I was ready to do something about it.

As I ran around getting ready for school the next morning, my phone beeped with a text. My heart was racing and I was smiling as I dug through my bag and finally found it. Clearly one of my friends had come to her senses and made the first move!

The text was from Bri. "U r getting Missy and Hattie 2day. Don't forget."

The smile slid off my face as I glared at my phone. I didn't need her acting like my mom, nagging me about something that I could remember just fine without her. "I know," I texted back. "Don't need a reminder."

I stomped to school, waiting for a snippy reply, and sure enough it came as I reached the sidewalk in front of the building. "You forgot the last time it was your turn to get them."

The familiar coal of anger burned hot as I texted back. "It was one time," I replied, my fingers flying over my screen as the warning bell rang. I had more to say but I couldn't be late. I turned my phone off—the last thing I needed was it ringing in school and getting confiscated—and flew up the stairs, angrier than ever.

How could I have ever, for one second, thought I missed someone as maddening as Bri?

10

"Sasha, would you get that ball, please?" Kim asked me, looking toward me but not actually at me. I wasn't sure what was weirdest: the way she said "Sasha" instead of "Sash," the fact that she said "please," or how cold her voice was. But I knew I hated all three.

"Yes," I replied, my voice just as chilly as I grabbed the tennis ball that had landed near my feet.

I saw Tim and Caley exchange a puzzled look. It

wasn't their first of the afternoon. I'd arrived at the shelter half an hour ago with Missy and Hattie and could easily say it was our worst club meeting ever. It was really hard to be part of a club where none of the members were speaking to each other unless they absolutely had to.

Taylor's back was to the rest of us as she snuggled with Missy and Humphrey. Bri was throwing a blue ball for Boxer, Hattie, Jinx, and Daisy, acting like Kim, Taylor, and I were invisible. Kim and Caley had Violet, Waffles, Lily, and Gus playing with tennis balls and I was on the floor with Mr. S, who had come over the second he saw me and not left my side since. He could tell how bad I felt and I loved that he came to snuggle with me. Still, this was his playtime and I wanted him to have fun with the other dogs, so after tossing the tennis ball back to Kim (a bad throw since I wasn't looking at her either) I stood up. Big Al and Gracie were in the front corner with a rubber bone, so I headed toward them with Mr. S, snagging a green ball on my way.

"Let's play," I told the three dogs, throwing the ball into the corner farthest away from any of my friends-who-weren't-my-friends. Mr. S and Gracie flew after the ball but Big Al looked up at me, eyes wide, as if asking whether it was safe to chase it.

"Go get it, big guy," I encouraged, and after a moment the little dog took off after his friends. I couldn't help grinning at that. The people in this club might be upset but at least the dogs were their usual adorable selves. And it was good to see Big Al coming more and more out of his shell.

But an hour later even the dogs were no longer themselves. They'd probably picked up on the tension between the humans because by now even Tim and Caley were clearly on edge from our weird behavior. Boxer was short tempered, Big Al had gone to hide in his cage, and every time someone threw a ball, the dogs were pushy with each other as they ran for it.

Violet was particularly snarly and Kim was staying close to her, which had earned her a few nasty looks from Bri. But Kim held her head high as she worked with the Dalmatian to keep her calm and out of trouble with the other dogs.

But then Tim threw Boxer's Frisbee a bit too close to Violet, who grabbed it and gave a low growl when Boxer trotted up. Lily was right behind him and the fur on her neck rose as Boxer's tiny ears flattened. Bri headed over to Lily and began to soothe her. Kim was trying to coax Violet to release the Frisbee, which made Bri roll her eyes, but Violet was having none of it and Boxer was getting distressed. Tim went over to help but accidently stepped on Gus's tail and had to stop to comfort him. So I headed over to Boxer instead—but Taylor had the same idea and we both got to the big dog at the same time. I glared at her and she glared right back and while neither of us was looking, Boxer snapped at Violet.

"Yikes," Tim said as Gus scurried off to the side. "Careful."

Taylor took a step back.

"Should we get Boxer away from Violet?" Caley asked anxiously.

"Yes, and let's all stay calm," Kim advised, earning another eye roll from Bri. "It doesn't help anything if we get worked up." Though I could tell by the tightness around her mouth that she was worried as she stepped away from the dogs and headed for the supply cabinet.

Bri coaxed Lily away while I tried to get Boxer's attention with a tennis ball. He was too focused on Violet to notice me. And I had to admit the way his little ears were flat and he growled ominously scared me a bit.

"Boxer, come," I called, trying to sound firm. But my voice wobbled and Boxer ignored me.

Then he took a step toward Violet and barked loudly. Alice popped out of her office looking concerned. "What's going on?" she asked.

"Guys," Caley called in a warning tone.

But then Kim was between the dogs, a box of treats in hand. At the scent of their favorite snack, both dogs dropped their aggressive stances and became the sweet pups we knew, both eager for a biscuit.

Kim handed one to me and I used it to lure Boxer to the other side of the room. Then she shook the box enticingly and led Violet to a quiet corner. Bri began playing tug-of-war with Lily, far from both Violet and Boxer. Taylor headed over to a group of dogs who were in the middle of the room looking confused by everything.

"Are we okay now?" Alice asked. Her T-shirt of the day was one of her funny ones, three dogs sunbathing under the words "Hot Dogs," but her expression was serious.

"Yes, fine," Taylor said quickly. Gracie brought a tennis ball over to her and Taylor threw it across the room with a bit too much force, causing it to bounce wildly.

"Violet's calmed down," Kim reported from where she and Violet were snuggling on the floor, Violet still crunching her treat. Hattie had come over to join them.

"Boxer too," I said. The big dog had settled down, so I went over to check on Big Al.

"Kim saved the day," Tim said in a jovial voice.

Bri snorted from her corner of the room.

Alice looked over at her and Bri's cheeks turned pink, but her lips were pressed together in a thin line.

"So we're all good?" Alice asked, looking from Bri to Kim and then to me and Taylor.

"Totally fine," Bri said stiffly.

"Let me know if you need anything then," Alice said. She lingered a moment longer, clearly not convinced all was well.

But then the shelter door opened and Mrs. Washington came in, followed by Mrs. Torres, Daisy's owner. Pickup had started, so any more conversation would have to wait, thank goodness.

"Sasha, I had something to ask you," Mrs. Torres said, coming up to where I was petting Big Al, who glanced at her fearfully. Mrs. Torres, a retired teacher who did volunteer work while Daisy was at the club, smiled down at him and held out a hand for him to sniff. He hesitated, touched his nose to her palm delicately, and then allowed her to stroke his head. I had only spoken to Mrs. Torres in passing, since she dropped Daisy off at the club and rarely needed to reschedule, but seeing this exchange made it clear she was a devoted dog person.

"Sure," I said, standing up. "What can I do for you?"

"My son is visiting from Portland next week," she said. "So I was hoping I could arrange for pickup service for Daisy on Wednesday."

"Absolutely," I said. "I'll make a note of it and Alice will put the extra fee on your monthly bill for the club. You can give us a key or leave one at the house under a flowerpot or something. And please make sure we can find Daisy's leash."

"I'll just give you the key now if that's all right," she said, taking an envelope out of her purse and handing it to me. "And I keep the leash on a hook right by the door."

"Okay, then I think we're set," I said. "I'll pick up Daisy myself." That would be easier than asking Kim, Taylor, or Bri to do it. It was hard to ask them to do anything when we weren't speaking. And it would be fun to walk Daisy to the meeting and spend a bit of time with her outside the shelter.

"Sounds good," she said, nodding. "Thank you."

"What are you and your son going to do while he's here?" I asked as we walked toward the front door. Most of the dogs had been picked up and it was time for me and Mr. S to head home too.

"We're going to see my sister in Germantown," she said. "And eat lunch at Café DuBois."

Germantown was about an hour away and even I had heard of Café DuBois, a fancy restaurant that had been written up in national papers.

"That sounds really fun," I said as Mr. S bounded up to me. He was ready to go out again. "And yummy."

She was smiling as she snapped Daisy's leash on. "He's a chef, so he wanted to try their cuisine. Thanks

142

again for walking Daisy so I can enjoy the day with my son. I don't get to see him very often."

"We'll take great care of Daisy," I promised as she waved and then headed out.

I reached for my backpack, which was hanging on a rack by the door, intending to make a note in my phone about getting Daisy on Wednesday. But just as I got ahold of it, Bri grabbed hers and our hands bumped. Bri snatched her arm away as though touching me might give her some kind of horrible disease. I glared at her, then took my bag and heaved it over my shoulders.

"Careful," Taylor said coldly. She was standing right behind me and I'd nearly hit her in the face.

Normally I would have apologized but today I just ignored her. I heard Kim cough as I marched for the door, possibly in reaction to the way Bri had thrown open the door and stormed out with Lily. But I didn't look back. It felt weird and awkward and downright awful to leave the club alone. Even Mr. S glanced back toward the shelter and then up at me, as if to ask where our friends were.

"They're not our friends right now," I told him. And the two of us headed home alone.

We hadn't planned a sleepover that weekend because Taylor was going to an old friend's bat mitzvah in North Carolina, Kim's family was going out to dinner on Saturday to celebrate Matt's birthday, and Bri had plans with her parents since her dad was home. Saturday I would be at the dance studio all day, but before the fight Kim and I had decided to spend Sunday at my house working on our reports for social studies.

I would have slept in on Sunday morning—I was worn out from rehearsal the day before and I'd been having trouble falling asleep ever since the big fight. But Mr. S had no plans to let me stay in bed a moment longer than usual. Which would have been annoying, but it's hard to be annoyed at being woken up with sweet doggy kisses.

"You're the cutest little guy in the world," I told him as I dragged myself out of bed.

He barked happily, maybe agreeing with me or maybe just pleased that his day was starting. No matter how exhausted I was in the morning, Mr. S made me smile, with all his energy and enthusiasm. He pranced around the block on our walk, taking time to give me kisses as we went. Then back at the house he frisked about as I padded into the kitchen to give him breakfast. And after wolfing that down, he let out a contented sigh and came to lie at my feet for his first nap of the day.

"You have a good life," I told him, rubbing his tummy with my foot. I was at the table eating oatmeal that my mom, who had come downstairs while I was out, had made for us.

"I think that dog is spoiled," my mom said, grinning. She looked sleepy too since she'd been out late at another work dinner. She'd mentioned that Taylor's dad was there but I hadn't asked more about it. I wasn't interested in Taylor right now.

"Mr. S isn't spoiled, he's just happy," I said.

My mom gave him an affectionate pat as she got up to take her dish into the kitchen. "We should all be so happy," she said. "What are your plans for the day, Sash?"

"I'm going to work on my social studies project," I said, trying to keep my voice even as my stomach scrunched up into a tight ball. I wasn't sure if Kim was still planning to come over. She probably wasn't, of course. But I had to admit that a tiny part of me hoped she would. Maybe if the two of us talked alone, she'd apologize and we'd figure out a way to make things work between all four of us.

"No friends today?" my mom asked.

"I don't know," I said, pushing the last bite of oatmeal around my bowl instead of eating it. It was hard to eat with a scrunched-up stomach.

Now my mom was looking at me quizzically. "You don't know?" she repeated, sounding more like a lawyer than a mom.

"Well, it's just people are out of town and Kim wasn't sure if she could come over to study with me," I said quickly. I ducked my head so that my curls, which I hadn't had time to put up yet, fell over my face. I didn't need my mom, with her honed instincts for exposing liars on the witness stand, seeing my guilty expression.

"Hm," my mom said. She was probably about to say more but her phone rang, thank goodness.

"That was a close call," I whispered to Mr. S, who wriggled slightly but didn't open his eyes.

"Good morning, Jon," my mom said in a voice that was very different from the one she'd just been using to interrogate me. It was filled with laughter, almost giddy really. Jon was Taylor's dad. He was a pretty funny guy and had probably cracked a joke. As if to confirm this, my mom let out a peal of laughter. I realized I missed Taylor's dad and his jokes, and her sisters, and Kim's family too. I used to go over to Kim's almost every day after school. That was back in elementary school, before

147

we had loads of homework and two extra friends hanging out with us. For a moment I sighed, thinking about how things were easier back then.

But as my mom laughed again, I realized it wasn't a good time for a walk down memory lane; it was a good time to make my escape while she was distracted. I rinsed my bowl in the sink, put it in the dishwasher, and headed upstairs. My phone was on my desk and I checked to see if there were any messages. When it lit up I saw that there was one: a text from Kim.

My heart beat slightly faster as I picked it up and read, "Can't meet today. I have a cold."

A wave of disappointment washed over me, followed by one of irritation. If she wanted to cancel she could have come up with a better excuse. I debated what to write back—"No problem"? "I was busy anyway"? Nothing seemed right. So in the end I didn't reply at all. Instead I sat down in front of my pile of books about Mongolia, determined to finish the last of my research.

But I only made it about halfway through: I was too busy fretting about my friends-who-were-no-longer-my-friends to focus on anything.

"Nice work today," Madame Florence told me as we wrapped up our final private rehearsal. "You are ready to perform."

Her praise made me warm inside, like a hot cup of cocoa on an icy day. It *had* been an icy week, actually, with my friends not speaking at all. The club meeting yesterday had been the worst: we arranged all the pick-ups through texts and then barely looked at each other when we were at the shelter. By the end of the afternoon Tim and Caley were doing everything they could to get us talking, not that it worked.

"Thanks," I told Madame Florence. "I'm excited."

"You should be," my teacher said with a rare smile.

I was smiling myself as I walked toward the dressing room, my footsteps echoing slightly in the empty hall. As I passed the reception desk I saw a pile of flyers for the show that weekend and my chest fluttered with anticipation. I imagined being onstage at the town hall auditorium, where the performance would be taking place, with my friends cheering me on from the front row. And then my smile slipped away. Because things were still bad with my friends. Awful, really. And I was tired of it.

I headed over to my locker, stripped out of my sweaty dance clothes, and put on my school clothes. It was when I was tying my shoes that I decided enough was enough. I needed my friends and they needed me too.

It was time to end this fight once and for all, and I knew the time to do it was tomorrow, at the Wednesday meeting of our Dog Club.

11

All day at school I thought about the fight. I realized I was upset about two things: the fact that I did more work than anyone else for the club, and the way my friends had made it seem like it was my fault, because I was so disorganized. So I concocted a plan. I'd be first at our club meeting that afternoon, to show them how responsible and organized I was, and then I'd explain that it was time to rethink the division of labor for the club. I'd be calm and state the facts, the way my mom did in a big case. And I was sure my friends would agree and probably also be impressed with how organized my argument was. It would be a win–win.

When the final bell rang I raced out of school to pick up Mr. S, Popsicle, and Humphrey. I reviewed my argument in my mind as I leashed up each of the dogs and the four of us headed into town. A slight rain started falling as we nearly ran down Main Street. I waved at Kim's mom, who was at the host desk in the Rox, and my stomach rumbled when I passed Sugar and Spice with its delicious scent of chocolate, lemon, and cinnamon wafting out. But there was no stopping for a treat today. I was going to be first at the shelter no matter what.

Except that I wasn't: Bri was already there, unclipping Missy and Hattie from their leashes, when I came in, breathless and damp from the rain.

"Oh," I said as I nearly stepped on Bri.

"Watch it," she said, her mouth all pinched up.

"I—" I began, but Bri had already started walking away, her back to me and her spine ramrod straight.

Okay, fine, I wouldn't start with her. But I had to admit my feelings of goodwill were curdling as I toweled off my three charges and sent them to play.

Caley came in, shaking out her umbrella. Today her red hair was up in a high bun that I suspected was a sock bun because it was so perfect and fat. This was not something I would have known before I met Bri, who was always sharing hair tips with us—a thought I pushed away because I did not want to think about crabby Bri.

"Bad news," Caley said, smoothing the bun, which was still sleek and perfect after her long day at school. "Tim is sick today so it's just going to be us holding down the fort."

That was bad news, with the rest of us not speaking to each other.

"We'll miss him," Alice said. She'd come out of her office to say hi and was petting Oscar in his cat bed.

Today she wore a shirt that had a set of human footprints next to a set of paw prints and a slogan on top that said "Happy Together." "But it's been a pretty smooth day so far. Once we get the dogs playing we'll be fine."

I looked around the shelter to see which dogs I could get playing. Big Al and Gracie were in a corner sniffing at the toy bin and I headed over to help them find something fun. Caley began a game of fetch with Popsicle, Hattie, and Boxer, while Missy and Humphrey greeted each other and then trotted around the shelter, clearly trying to decide what to do together.

I wasn't sure what Bri was doing because I didn't even feel like looking in her direction after she'd been so unpleasant.

I was digging through the toy bin looking for a Frisbee when Kim came in with Jinx and Gus. I tried to catch her eye and smile, to get things moving toward a reconciliation, but she avoided looking around at all. She just let her dogs free and then went to check on Violet, who was in her cage.

I stood up, thinking maybe I'd walk by and check on Violet too, but just then Taylor came in and a big gust of wind blew the door out of her hands and into the wall behind it with a loud thud.

Big Al raced for cover under his blanket, Missy cowered behind Humphrey, and Violet looked out suspiciously from the doorway of her cage.

"Sorry," Taylor said sheepishly as Alice hurried out of her office to see what was wrong.

"I guess it's getting pretty stormy out there," Alice said, going over to free Waffles and Lily from their leashes while Taylor closed the door.

"Yeah, it's really coming down," Taylor said, shrugging out of her wet coat and hanging it up.

The moment Lily was free she ran over to greet Bri, who was now playing with Boxer and Mr. S. After Bri had snuggled Lily, she threw the tennis ball across the shelter where it came close to Violet. Violet stepped out of her cage, picked up the ball, and began to run. It seemed like we were all holding our breath as she came back to Bri, dropped the ball at her feet, and got jostled by Boxer, who wanted his turn.

Sure enough, Violet's ears flattened. Boxer took a step back and Kim rushed over. But before touching Violet she looked at Bri and arched a brow. "Do I need to ask your permission to help?" she asked frostily.

Bri's eyes narrowed and I saw Alice and Caley exchange a tired look.

"Why bother when you know it all?" Bri muttered, too low for Alice and Caley to hear. But Kim's mouth pressed into a firm line as she led Violet away.

Taylor, who had also heard, rolled her eyes, and I let out a sigh. Clearly no one was in the mood to apologize, so it didn't make sense to try and talk now. I'd finally uncovered a Frisbee, which I sent flying across the room, Popsicle, Jinx, and Gus racing after it. I'd wait until things got better and then explain my argument to my friends.

But then things got worse. Violet growled at any dog that came near her, but still wanted to play fetch, so that happened a lot. We were all cooped up because of the rain, and since we still weren't speaking to one another, no one wanted to start a group game. By the time pickup rolled around, Caley's sock bun was falling apart, Bri's neat braids were frizzy, Kim's face was flushed, and Taylor looked ready for a long nap.

Mrs. Washington arrived first and Gus rushed up to greet her. A moment later Mrs. Torres walked in wearing a snazzy plastic raincoat and matching rain hat. She was smiling as she ushered in a young man with warm brown eyes and a sloping nose that looked just liked hers.

"This is my son, Ricardo," I heard her say proudly to Caley, who was near the door snuggling with Hattie.

That rang a bell, but I wasn't quite sure why. I also wasn't sure why Daisy wasn't rushing up to meet Mrs. Torres the way she usually did.

"Nice to meet you," Caley said, going over to shake Ricardo's hand. "And let's see about Daisy. It's been so hectic I'm not sure where she is."

Then, in a sickening rush, I remembered our conversation last week, the one where Mrs. Torres had asked me to pick up Daisy this afternoon. The one I had totally forgotten until now.

My mouth was dry as I rushed up to her. The smile was fading from her lips as she looked around, trying to find her dog.

"Mrs. Torres, I'm so sorry," I said, feeling like I might choke on the words. "I forgot to get Daisy."

Mrs. Torres drew in a sharp breath. "So she's been alone at home this whole time?"

"I'm so sorry," I repeated, squeezing my fingers together so tightly they hurt.

Kim, who was standing nearby with Violet, looked at me, shocked, and Taylor came up behind me. "We were supposed to get Daisy today?" she asked.

"Yes, I spoke to Sasha about it last week," Mrs. Torres said in a clipped voice. "We'd better get home to check on her right away, Ricardo."

Her son nodded and the two of them swept out.

I knew this had ruined the end of their special day together and I felt horrible as I watched them go.

Alice had come out of her office and her face was solemn. "Sasha, what happened?" she asked in a voice so serious it made me wince.

"I just, I forgot," I stammered. "I have all this stuff for school and then there's my dance recital. I know it's no excuse, though. I should have remembered. Mrs. Torres was counting on me."

"Yes, she was," Alice said in a resigned tone. She looked at the door for a moment, then started back to her office. "I'll call and leave a message asking her to let us know how Daisy's doing when she gets home."

Kim opened her mouth to speak but before she could, Bri strode up and glared at me. "So we were supposed to pick up Daisy today and you didn't tell any of us?"

I glared right back. She knew full well why I hadn't told any of them: we weren't speaking.

"Club business should be more important than

anything else," Bri said, her hands now on her hips. "You had a responsibility to let us know we were supposed to pick up an extra dog this week."

"And a responsibility to Daisy," Kim said. Her voice wasn't quite as biting as Bri's but I could see she was upset at the thought of poor Daisy being locked up all day.

"I know," I said miserably. I was just as upset about Daisy and about letting down Mrs. Torres as they were, maybe even more—couldn't they see that? "I messed up and I'm sorry."

"You're always sorry, but you keep messing up anyway," Bri pointed out bluntly. She flicked her braid over her shoulder as if to emphasize her point.

"That's because I have too much to do," I said between clenched teeth. "It's impossible to stay on top of it all."

"It's not impossible if you take the time to organize everything," Bri said, her voice getting louder.

"Calm down or you'll upset Violet," Kim said,

glancing to where Violet lay on the floor near Boxer and Lily. All three dogs were looking at us uneasily.

"Right, of course I will, because that's what I do, upset the dogs," Bri said sarcastically. "And nothing else, because I'm not even a real part of this club."

"We should all try to stay calm," Taylor said, glancing at Caley, who was looking over at us with concern.

"That's not what I said!" Kim exclaimed, now speaking even louder than Bri and completely ignoring Taylor. Her face was flushed and her eyes were flashing.

"Bri just likes to blame everyone else for things," I said primly. "Instead of actually stepping up and helping."

"I wanted to help with Violet!" she shouted.

Kim threw up her arms. "Then why did you just stand there waiting for me to step in?" she fumed.

"Because you didn't give me a chance," Bri hissed.

"Right, everything is always someone else's fault," I said.

Bri spun around to try and stare me down. "At least

I'm not the one who stranded a dog at home and let the owner down. If you keep going like this you're going to destroy the club."

"Maybe if we just—" Taylor began, but I interrupted.

"The club that I helped found?" I shouted, furious and hurt by her words. "The one that I spend hours working on every day while you just sit around whining?"

Boxer barked, clearly worked up by all the tension and yelling. Caley went over to soothe him but she glanced back at us warily.

"Guys," Taylor pleaded. "Let's try to talk about this quietly." She was patting Jinx, who was looking at all of us with big eyes.

"That's not going to help anything," Bri said, throwing out her arms.

Hattie, who had been standing behind her, backed away, nearly bumping into Gracie, who growled, which was totally unlike her.

"No, but you insulting all of us will?" I countered. That coal of anger was burning white-hot in my stomach and my fists were clenched. Mr. S came up to me and leaned against my leg.

"At least I say what I think," Bri said, glaring at Taylor. She had a point: I was tired of how Taylor kept telling everyone to calm down but never actually helped out.

"Well, we're all sick of hearing what you think," Kim snapped in a very un-Kimlike way that made Missy let out a slight whine. Humphrey heard and howled.

"Too bad because—" Bri began loudly.

But then Alice strode in between us and held up her hands. "Enough," she said in a forceful voice that reminded us who the ultimate dog whisperer was. "You're scaring the dogs."

I looked around and saw that every dog in the shelter was still, all of them staring at us. I couldn't even see Big Al because he was hiding in his cage and Missy was cowering in a corner. Alice was right: the dogs were totally freaked out by all the yelling.

Guilt ballooned inside me and my shoulders slumped, the fight gone out of me. It was bad enough that I'd let down Mrs. Torres—now we were all being completely unprofessional. And the worst part was that the dogs that we loved so much were frightened. They were scared by the very people who were supposed to be taking care of them: us. How could we have let this happen?

"This is not the first meeting that has been disrupted by whatever is going on between you," Alice said. "It's interfering with our care for the dogs and it can't continue."

I started to apologize for the millionth time, but Alice went on. "Take the weekend to think about where you want to go from here," she said, her voice sober. "If you think you can work together again, by all means come back. But until you're ready to put the dogs and their needs first, you need to take a break from the club."

Her words hit me like a punch.

"Owners are arriving," Alice continued. "And we don't want them seeing their pets anxious and the people they trust to care for those pets shouting at each other. The four of you should go home. Now."

Alice had never gotten angry with us before and it felt awful. My hands were shaking as I leashed Mr. S and grabbed my coat and backpack. Kim was stuffing her arms into the sleeves of her fleece jacket and I saw that her lips were trembling. Bri kept her eyes down as she snapped Lily into her leash and Taylor led the way toward the door. I could tell by the tight expression on her face that she was trying not to cry.

The evening was cold and an icy drizzle fell from a low, gray sky. Bri pulled Lily ahead and marched toward her block, not pausing to look at us or say a word. Taylor glanced at me and then Kim. Her eyes were moist and for a moment I thought she might say something. But then she just turned and started for home, her hands jammed into the pockets of her coat.

I turned to Kim. Maybe if we could talk we could somehow fix this terrible mess. But Kim just gave me a hard look and then stomped down the block.

I looked down at Mr. S and felt tears start in a slow trickle down my face. "I guess I really blew that," I told him, sniffing as I spoke.

Mr. S gave a sympathetic yip but even he couldn't make me feel better now.

Because if we didn't fix this and fix it soon, it would mean the end of the Dog Club.

12

"Excellent work, dancers," Madame Florence said. It was Thursday afternoon and we had just finished up our final dress rehearsal in the studio. Tomorrow afternoon we'd do one last run-through in the auditorium itself. "You are more than ready for the performance on Saturday. And I'm happy to announce that our tickets have sold out. We're going to have a full house for what I know will be a wonderful show.

So give yourselves a hand."

All the dancers around me whooped and cheered. Asha and Dana did a jumping high five, while a few members of the advanced modern class did an impromptu jig across the floor that made even stoic Madame Florence laugh.

The only person not laughing or cheering or even smiling was me. I wanted to, of course. We'd worked so hard and earned this moment of fun together. Plus it was a great way to let off steam before the pressure of a performance. But it was impossible to feel happy after what had happened at Dog Club yesterday.

When I'd gotten home from the shelter I'd explained my splotchy face and lack of appetite as nerves about dance. My mom seemed slightly suspicious but then she'd had to answer a call from work and I'd gone upstairs and stayed in my room for the rest of the night. The one good thing that happened was that when I called Mrs. Torres to check on Daisy and apologize again, she had been kind, saying that she understood, that Daisy was fine, and that she was looking forward to the next Dog Club session. I'd breathed a sigh of relief that Mrs. Torres wasn't pulling Daisy from the club. But if things didn't get fixed soon, there might not be a club for Daisy to come back to.

And that made it impossible to be happy about anything.

"Sasha, are you okay?" Dana asked, her brow furrowed with concern. The other dancers were dispersing now, laughing and talking as they milled toward the dressing room.

I forced a smile, but it felt stiff on my face. "I'm a little nervous about the show," I said.

"I get that," Asha said, slinging an arm around my shoulders. "You have a major solo."

"Don't make it worse for her," Dana said. She was rolling out her shoulders to loosen them up after the intensity of our rehearsal.

"It's okay," I said. "We've practiced so much I think I could do it in my sleep. I just need to remember that when I picture the auditorium filled with people." We headed over to put our costumes for the last dance in the bins at the back of the room. For each of our numbers in the show we wore our own basic black leotard and tights, and then added fun accessories, like sparkly silver vests, colorful swirly skirts, and for the final number, butterfly wings.

"Yeah, it's pretty cool we're going to have a full house," Asha said, setting her wings, which were a shimmery blue and lavender, carefully in their bin. "That's a lot of people."

"Make sure to tell Kim and Taylor and Bri to get there early for good seats," Dana said. "I think Emily, Naomi, and Rachel are planning to arrive around one thirty." The show started at two o'clock.

"That's when my friends and family are coming too," Asha added.

I was glad we were now walking to the dressing room so they couldn't see my expression. Because if my friends didn't even want to talk to me, why would they come see me dance? Or sleep over at my house afterward? The answer, of course, was that they wouldn't.

I half listened as Dana and Asha chatted while we changed, but my mind was playing back the way none of my friends had even looked at me during that day at school, our big fight yesterday, and the day before that. The reality was that whatever had gone wrong was not going to be better by the weekend.

And so before I headed out to meet my mom in the parking lot, I sent the hardest text I'd ever had to send. I canceled our sleepover for Saturday night.

I waited all night for my friends to write back, to protest, to say they would be there to see me dance no matter what.

But no one did.

I was in English class when I realized how badly I'd messed up. Mrs. Benson, looking polished in her pressed pants and white linen shirt, was lecturing us on *The*

Adventures of Huckleberry Finn, which we were reading as a follow-up to our unit on *The Adventures of Tom Sawyer.* I was writing down the main themes of the book when Mrs. Benson cleared her throat.

"One thing to remember in literature and life," she said, raising an eyebrow as she stared down at Jade, who was trying to pass a note to Sofia. Jade crunched up the paper, her cheeks turning pink. "Is that actions have consequences. And when we take those actions, we cannot always foresee what the consequences will be."

I wasn't sure if this was about the book or the note-passing, but her words made my pen freeze over my paper. I realized I'd been thinking about the fight and my friends' seeming indifference to my stress as things that had just happened to me, kind of like a rainstorm sweeping in or a big report being assigned when you already had too much going on: the kind of thing that you had no control over. But now I started thinking in Mrs. Benson's terms, about actions and consequences.

At first all I could see were my friends' actions: Kim

not really hearing me when I first tried to talk about how stressed I was, Bri nagging me, Taylor not doing anything to help. But then I realized part of the picture was missing. And that part was me. Because they weren't the only ones who had acted; I had too. And when I thought about it honestly, I saw that my actions had created the consequences just as much as anyone else's, if not more. I was the one who was upset about the division of jobs for the club, but instead of talking about it calmly, I'd blown up about it. It had bothered me for weeks, but instead of trying to sort it out, I'd stewed and gotten angrier and angrier until it exploded. And now here we were, with our friendship in tatters and the whole future of our club up in the air.

Mrs. Benson was back to *The Adventures of Huckleberry Finn*, but I wasn't even trying to listen anymore. My actions had helped cause this whole mess, and now it was time to act again. But this time I needed to clean things up.

★ ★ ★

I waited for my friends under the big maple tree on the front lawn of the school. It was the perfect place because everyone had to pass by it on their way out, after the final bell. I'd skipped going to my locker to make sure I was there before any of my friends had a chance to leave. That way I'd be sure to catch all three of them. I wasn't sure what I was going to say exactly, but I did know how I was going to begin: I was going to apologize.

Students spilled out of the big metal doors of the school in a steady stream, pairs of eighth-grade girls talking with their heads bent together, groups of seventh-grade boys laughing and shoving each other in a way that reminded me of Boxer, Lily, and Jinx when they ran after a ball together. I saw Dana leaving with Emily, Naomi, and Rachel, and she waved to me.

"See you at the auditorium," she called. Madame Florence had instructed us to go home and eat a healthy snack before heading over to the town hall auditorium at four for our final run-through.

"See you there," I called back, smiling. Because I was sure my friends and I would be friends again by then.

More students filed out. Jade and Sofia and the rest of their fashionable crowd strolled down the steps as if they were posing for a magazine and then a group of boys from our class crashed into them. There was a lot of yelling and in the end the boys walked off meekly. I kept my eyes on the students still coming out but didn't see my friends. Where could they be? The stream of students had now slowed to a trickle, and there was still no sign of them.

But then the door opened and there they were, all three of them, together. Bri was saying something and gesturing with her hands while Kim leaned forward, listening intently. Taylor brushed a braid back from her face, then nodded. They were so focused on their conversation that they didn't even see me standing there in front of the maple tree, alone.

My insides felt scraped out and raw as I watched

them walk to the end of the path together. Taylor said something and Kim and Bri laughed, the sound carrying in the wind. Tears pricked my eyes as they headed down the sidewalk, clearly having a great time without me. I'd been ready to be friends again and apparently so were they. The only difference is that they only wanted to be friends with each other and not with me.

Obviously I was right: my actions had caused all our problems. And now my best friends in the world didn't want to have anything to do with me.

13

"You're going to be great," Asha said. We were backstage at the Roxbury Park town hall auditorium and in exactly ten minutes our performance was going to begin. The seats were filled and we could hear the low hum of the people talking and rustling their programs. Madame Florence had finished taking us through our warm-up and given a stirring pep talk. Her eyes had darted over to me a number of times while she spoke and I'd seen concern flicker across her face each time. It was a lot like the concern I saw reflected in Asha's eyes as she tried to cheer me up now.

And I knew why: I'd been awful at our run-through yesterday. My lifts sagged, my spins dragged, and I couldn't stay on beat. Madame Florence had called it pre-performance jitters but I knew it had nothing to do with the show. Or jitters. It was the loss of my friends. I needed to feel joyful to dance and now, knowing my friends no longer wanted me had sucked every bit of joy away.

I gave Asha a wan smile. "You too," I said. She would be great, of course. Everyone would. And I knew I had to rally, to find some way to get through this recital without letting everyone down. They'd all worked too hard to have this day spoiled by one brokenhearted dancer. The problem was, I had no idea how to fly through my dance when I felt this heavy and low.

"They're here," Dana said, coming up with a big grin. She'd been peeking out through the thick velvet curtains. "And they got front-row seats."

"Great," I said, my voice thin. I knew she was happy to have Emily, Rachel, and Naomi there to cheer her on. I'd always loved having Kim there clapping for me. And I'd so been looking forward to having Taylor and Bri join her.

"Kim, Bri, and Taylor must have been the first ones in the door," Dana went on. "Because they're sitting front and center."

I was sure I'd misheard. "Wait, don't you mean Emily, Naomi, and Rachel?" I asked.

Dana nodded, slightly distracted by one of the backstage moms who had accidentally dropped the bin of butterfly wings. "Yeah, they're there too, right next to Kim," she said.

That couldn't be. My heart was fluttering faster than real butterfly wings as I tiptoed up to the curtain and pulled it back the tiniest bit. Sure enough, right there in the front row, each holding a bouquet of pink roses, were my friends. Kim's cheeks were bright with anticipation,

Bri had styled her hair in an elaborate twist, and Taylor had tucked an extra rose behind her ear. But the very best part of all? Each of them was wearing our T-shirt, the one that said "Roxbury Park Dog Club."

A huge grin took over my face, my heart so full of happiness I thought it might burst.

"All right, dancers, find your marks," Madame Florence called in a low voice.

I headed over to stage left, my feet light as feathers.

"Are you ready?" Asha whispered from her spot next to me.

I grinned. "Oh, yeah," I said.

Because now that I knew my friends were there for me and that our club would be okay, I was filled with so much joy I was beaming. And that meant I was ready to fly.

And fly I did. I soared across the stage, my spins glorious, my steps nimble, my timing perfect. I was radiant. I could feel it in every part of me as I leaped higher, twirled faster, and smiled bigger than I ever had before. And at the end of my solo, the audience rose up in a standing ovation. My friends were the first ones to their feet, Kim clapping hard, Bri doing a fist pump, and Taylor whistling loudly.

I bowed deeply and winked at Kim, Taylor, and Bri, who cheered even louder.

The moment the curtain fell after our final number, the celebration began. And this time I was right at the center of it, high-fiving my friends, laughing with everyone, and applauding when Madame Florence herself joined the impromptu dance led by the advanced modern class.

"We were awesome," Asha said, her eyes shining. "And your solo was incredible, Sasha. I've never seen you dance like that before. I mean, you're always good, but that was amazing."

"Thanks," I said, my insides fizzy with the euphoria that only came from dance—dance and my friends. "I think I had a little extra motivation."

"It was beautiful," Madame Florence said, coming up to us and resting a hand on my shoulder. Her cheeks were pink. "A flawless performance you should be proud of."

I glowed at her words.

Family and friends had started to stream backstage and I waved wildly when I saw Kim, Bri, and Taylor appear.

Kim flew over and wrapped me in a huge hug. Taylor threw her arms around both of us, and Bri did the same, though a bit more gingerly. "Careful not to crush the flowers, you guys," she said. "They're for the star and they need to be perfect."

"Kind of like you were perfect," Taylor said as she released me. "Sash, I knew you were good but I had no idea you were *this* good!"

"Seriously, you are so talented," Bri said, her voice tinged with awe.

"It was fantastic," Kim agreed, nodding.

"Thanks, you guys," I said, grinning and ducking my head. The praise felt good but also kind of overwhelming. "I'm so glad you were here." I looked back up at them so they could see how much it meant to me that they'd showed up despite everything.

The three of them exchanged a look.

"I can't believe we almost missed it because of a silly fight," Kim said, shaking her head slightly.

"Yeah, it all got so out of hand so fast," Bri said, looking slightly sheepish.

"But your text canceling the sleepover was the wake-up call we needed," Taylor said. "That's when we realized it was time to get our priorities straight."

"I feel like it's all my fault that it happened, though," I began.

But Taylor held up a hand. "I think we all have stuff to apologize for. But that can wait because I have to take some photos with the star!" She held up her camera.

"I want to be in it," Bri said, putting an arm around me and posing.

"Me too," Kim said, leaning in on my other side.

"How about a picture of all of you?" my mom

asked. I hadn't even seen her come backstage but she was beaming and leaned over to give me a kiss. "You were glorious," she said.

"Thanks," I said, thrilled at the way she smiled at me. After these past few weeks where all she could do was frown at my mistakes, it felt great to see her so proud.

Taylor set up the shot with the red velvet curtains as a backdrop and then handed her camera to my mom. The four of us wrapped our arms around each other.

"Say cheese," my mom said.

"I think we should say 'dance superstar,'" Taylor said.

"That's too long," Bri said, and I laughed. Bri could argue about anything. "How about just 'star'?"

"Or 'diva'?" Taylor asked, grinning. "Because that's what Sasha is."

But I knew the words that mattered most right now. They were way too long but not even Bri disagreed.

And so the four of us hugged each other, smiled big, and shouted, "Roxbury Park Dog Club forever!"

14

By the time we got back to my house for our sleepover we were starving. And of course my mom and I had not prepared the special dinner I'd hoped for.

"I'm sorry we always just have pizza at my sleepovers," I said after we'd placed our usual order with the Roxbury Park House of Pizza and headed up to my room. I was using my desk to stretch out my hamstrings, which were still a bit tight from dancing.

"Don't be silly," Bri said. She had dropped her overnight bag in the corner and was now on the floor snuggling with the dogs. Her mom had brought Lily over as soon as we'd gotten back so that the dogs could have their sleepover too. "I love pizza and I never get to eat it at home. Don't get me wrong—I love my mom's cooking. But sometimes a girl just wants some pepperoni in her life."

"I agree," Kim said. She was on the floor next to Bri rubbing Mr. S's belly. "My parents make great food but I need a pizza break sometimes too."

"Yeah, and since Jasmine stopped eating dairy last month, we never have pizza at my house either," Taylor added. "I've been looking forward to the pizza at your house for weeks. That was why I had to make sure we all became friends again, so I wouldn't miss out on my pizza night."

I laughed as Kim playfully swatted Taylor, who was lying on the bed, with a pillow. That got the dogs excited and Bri began playing tug-of-war with Mr. S while Kim and Taylor got out some chew toys for Lily.

As I stretched out my other leg I thought about what my friends had said. I'd just assumed that the pizza at my house was lame, but it turned out to be something my friends loved about coming over to my house. I'd been so sure the food was better at their houses that I'd almost messed up a tradition that they all looked forward to. It was another example of me not speaking up. And it was a mistake I didn't want to make again.

I perched on my desk and cleared my throat. "You guys, I need to apologize for getting so angry about the club," I said. "I do think we need to divide the work up differently, but I should have just talked to you guys about it as soon as I started feeling overwhelmed, instead of just staying quiet and getting more and more upset."

"Well, you did try to talk to me," Kim said with a sigh. "And I was so worried about my own stuff that I didn't really listen. So I'm sorry too."

"I'm sorry I got mad at you guys instead of telling you I wanted more responsibility in the club," Bri said, then turned to face Kim. "And that I yelled at you about Violet."

"I think I was taking over a lot," Kim said. Lily had come to sit on her lap and she rubbed the dog's furry belly gently. "But I shouldn't, because you are great with the dogs—all of you are."

"I need to watch the things I say, though," Bri said, the corners of her mouth turning down a bit. "And how I say them. I thought I was getting better but apparently not."

"No, you're a lot better than you used to be," Taylor said immediately, reaching over and patting Bri's shoulder. "Remember when you kept calling me *new girl* and dropped a smoothie on me on purpose? That was way worse."

Bri covered her head with her hands but she was laughing. "I still can't believe I was so mean," she said, her voice muffled. "How did you ever forgive me?"

"I'm just fabulously generous like that," Taylor said airily.

"So I guess I can feel good that I didn't pelt anyone with a fruit drink when I got angry this time," Bri said.

"We all appreciated that," Kim said, laughing. Lily licked her cheek, which made her laugh even more.

"Seriously though, you guys," Bri said as she patted Mr. S, "I'm sorry about my temper and not thinking before I speak. I really am working on it and I'll keep trying."

"We know," Taylor said. She was back on the bed, her braids spilling across my pillow. "And it's not like any one of us is perfect. Well, except me."

Bri snickered.

Taylor sighed theatrically. "Okay, I know I have things to be sorry about too. I should have listened to you more, Sasha, and worried less about trying to make everyone get along since it clearly didn't work at all."

Kim snickered at that. "It really didn't," she said.

"Okay, we're all sorry," I said. "Does that mean we all forgive each other?"

"Yes," Bri, Taylor, and Kim chorused.

"Okay," I said, smiling. "Me too. So no more apologizing."

"Wait, there's one more thing I'm sorry about," Bri said, heading over to her bag. She unzipped it, rummaged about a bit, and then pulled out a plastic container. When I saw what was inside I burst out laughing.

"I'm sorry I forgot your rainbow sprinkles," Bri said, presenting me with a brand-new box of them. "I will never host a sleepover without them again."

That night my milk shake looked like a liquid rainbow with all the sprinkles I put in. And it tasted delicious: creamy, crunchy, and sweet. The four of us had settled in the den on the green corduroy sofa, stuffed with pizza and finishing up our shakes. The dogs were drowsy after their dinner and were piled together in the corner next to the big bookcase. The TV was on the opposite wall, tucked into a cabinet because my mom claimed she didn't like it "looking" at her. But the den was the one casual room in our house, so the sofa was worn, the table a bit scuffed, and the rug even had a slight stain if you looked under the table. It was a good place to relax, especially with my friends and the dogs.

"Lily and Mr. S are so cute," Taylor said as we cooed over them. "I want to take a picture but I'm too full to get up."

"Tell me about it," Bri said, resting a hand on her belly. Her empty shake glass was next to Taylor's on the coffee table.

"So did you guys finish your social studies reports yet?" Taylor asked, looking at me and Kim.

Kim nodded but I shook my head. "I just haven't been able to focus," I said, my chest tightening as I remembered the one bad thing still hanging over me. "But it's due on Wednesday and I don't think I can finish it in time."

Kim rubbed her hands together. "Of course you can, because I'm going to share all of Anna's wisdom with you," she said. "And Anna is the best tutor ever, so we're both going to ace it."

"That would be great," I said, relieved at the thought of getting some help. I took the last sip of my shake, then set my glass down next to the others. "My problem is that I can't figure out how to organize it. I think if I figured that out I could finally just write it."

"The secret to organizing a report or an essay is making an outline," Kim said, snuggling deeper into the puffy sofa cushions as she spoke. "Anna got me to make one and it made the whole thing a million times easier. I was going to tell you about it last weekend but then I got that terrible cold and had to stay home."

"So you really were sick when you canceled?" I asked. I hadn't even considered that Kim might have actually been under the weather.

Kim nodded. "Yeah, don't you remember how I was coughing at school?"

I shook my head ruefully. "I was too worried about my problems to notice anyone else's," I said.

Taylor held up a finger. "No more apologizing," she reminded me.

I laughed.

"I'll show you how to do the outline tomorrow morning," Kim promised me. "And then you'll have all day to work on the report. You'll get it done."

With her help I probably would—and that was an incredible relief. I sank back on the sofa with a contented sigh.

"And now we just need to restructure our Dog Club," Kim went on. "So that everybody has something to do and no one has too much to do."

So that's exactly what we did.

Monday afternoon the sun shone bright and an invigorating breeze carried the scent of crisp fall leaves. The trees were a brilliant red and gold as the four of us left school together, the way it was supposed to be.

"So Taylor's getting Jinx and Gus, Kim's getting Popsicle, Humphrey, and Mr. S, Sasha's picking up Missy and Hattie, and I'll get Waffles and Lily," Bri said, after consulting the calendar on her phone. On

Saturday we'd decided that Bri would be in charge of the club calendar, taking note of special pickups and doing a daily reminder of who was getting which dogs. We'd all agreed it was a necessary job and that Bri was the best one of us to do it.

"Any emails from potential clients?" Kim asked Taylor. We'd also decided that from now on we'd tell people interested in the club to email instead of call. That way we wouldn't waste so much time on the phone. Taylor was in charge of the emails and getting back to people about their spot on the wait list.

Taylor was checking her phone as well and she nodded. "Yeah, two," she said, then tucked her phone away. "I'll write them back later." That was one of the good things about emails—we could choose a good time to write back instead of letting club business interfere with actual club meetings. We'd all agreed that from now on, time with the dogs came first.

"And I'll call the Golds and the Santagelos later this week," I said, scuffing through a small pile of leaves on the sidewalk. We'd decided it was time to bring in the new club members, and calling new clients was still my job. It would be a lot more manageable since I wasn't doing all the other stuff on top of it. And I'd realized that while lately I'd been on the phone too much, when it wasn't overwhelming, it was something I really liked to do.

"It will be fun to expand the club," Kim said happily. "And I think Violet's ready. She can still get a bit snarly but she's settled in a lot."

"And I think all the dogs will be calmer now that we're getting along," Taylor added.

"Definitely," I agreed. Us getting along was better for everyone, that was for sure.

We had reached the corner where we would part ways to pick up our dogs.

"See you guys there," Bri said, waving as we headed off.

Twenty minutes later we were standing in front of the shelter, the dogs happily greeting each other with a lot of sniffing, yips, and jumping. We'd agreed it was important that we all go in together, to apologize for the mess of the last two weeks and promise it would never happen again. But the second we walked in, Violet, Gracie, and Boxer rushed over and there was a frenzy of happy barking and doggy hijinks as we let the club dogs off their leashes and everyone, human and dog, greeted each other.

Bri was hugging Violet, Kim was cuddling Big Al and Missy, Taylor was picking up the ball Waffles had rushed to drop at her feet, and I was on the floor with Hattie, Daisy, and Gus all trying to get on my lap when I heard someone laughing.

I looked up and saw Alice in her Roxbury Park Dog Club shirt, which matched the ones Taylor, Bri, Kim, and I were wearing. She took in the shirts, the dogs, and the four of us, and she nodded. "I see we're back," she said.

"Yes," I said, struggling to stand. "And we're sorry, Alice, and you too, Caley and Tim."

"We let things get out of hand and it won't ever happen again," Kim added seriously.

Tim gave us a thumbs-up and Caley grinned.

Alice looked at all of us warmly. "Glad to hear it," she said. "And I'm glad the Roxbury Park Dog Club is back how it belongs. Because these dogs have been waiting all day to play with you."

And who were we to keep them waiting?

Tim got out the basket for a game of doggy basketball, Bri began arguing with him about teams, Taylor headed over for the orange ball, and Kim coaxed Big Al to come over and give the game a try while I just took a moment to take it all in.

Because nothing in the world could make me happier than this: the dogs, my friends, and the Roxbury Park Dog Club!